TEAS FOR TINSEL AND OTHER STORIES

A HOLIDAY MYSTERY COLLECTION

HAUNTED TEAROOM COZY MYSTERIES

KAREN SUE WALKER

Published by Laragray Press

CONTENTS

TEA IS FOR TRICKS

1. Tea is for Tricks 3
2. Mummy Hot Dogs 41

TEA IS FOR TRADITION

1. Present Time 45
2. 1961 51
3. Present Time 77
4. Gelatin Pretzel Salad 79

TEA IS FOR TINSEL

1. Christmas in Serenity Cove 85
2. Mrs. Higglesworth and Miss Paisley 99
3. Whisk 105
4. Tiny 111
5. Chef Emile 115
6. The Ghost of Christmas Past 119
7. The Ghost of Christmas Presents 123
8. The Ghost of Christmas Future 131
9. A New Day Dawns 137
10. Christmas Eve Feast 145

Snowball Cookies 157

About the Author 159

Also by Karen Sue Walker 161

TEA IS FOR TRICKS

A HAUNTED TEAROOM HALLOWEEN
STORY

Fog drifted in from the ocean, settling around the base of my hundred-year-old Victorian home. On this Halloween night, even the moon participated in creating the perfect atmosphere by casting an eerie glow.

I dimmed the lights to set the mood and began pouring glasses of champagne. For the last night of the Haunts of Serenity Cove Tour, I'd planned a gourmet reception along with plenty of chills and thrills.

The house had originally been built as two residences, each floor with full living quarters and a full-sized kitchen. I lived on the second floor, along with my assistant and tenant Jennifer. I'd converted the first floor into a tearoom where I served tea, scones, and dainty sandwiches.

Jennifer descended the staircase wearing an exquisite, off-the-shoulder, 1950s gown, her hair pulled up into an elegant French twist. She gave a little curtsy. "What do you think, April?" A rhinestone necklace sparkled on her neck.

I grinned. "You look perfect."

The wind rattled the door, and I turned to see the tour guide leading her guests up the sidewalk like a mother duck with her progeny.

"Upstairs, quick." I gestured for Jennifer to hurry. She'd make her dramatic entrance later.

Hoping to have a quick word with my resident ghost, I ducked into the kitchen. I'd been trying to recruit him to add some spooky ambiance to the evening. What was the point of having your very own ghost if you couldn't get him to rattle some chains or emit mournful moans? Alas, Chef Emile Toussaint, a French chef who'd died sixty years previously, was nowhere to be found.

I hurried to greet Lois, the tour guide. Her twenty-something assistant, Andrew, held the door open for the others. His dark hair fell across his forehead, a put-upon expression on his face. He gave me a forced smile when he caught me watching him.

Tonight's guests wore costumes in honor of the holiday. One couple, in doctor and nurse outfits, would never be mistaken for the real thing. The blonde nurse's "uniform" barely covered her essential assets. She'd pinned a name tag to her chest that read, "Nurse Bambi."

Another couple put a halfhearted effort into their witch and warlock costumes, both dressed all in black with pointy hats. The warlock's beard appeared to have been made from a mop, but who was I to judge?

Two gray-haired ladies came through the door last, moving slowly. One wore a robe and slippers with stuffed cats of all different sizes pinned to her. The other, a frail woman in a bright pink evening gown and a "Miss America 1962" sash, pushed a walker in front of her.

"Nice costume," Bambi said to the woman in the robe. "What are you supposed to be? Someone too cheap to buy a real costume?"

The woman grinned. "I'm a crazy cat lady." She gave Bambi the once over. "How lovely the strip club gave you the night off."

Bambi turned to the young man next to her, and whispered, "Did she just insult me?"

"Let's begin, shall we?" I said as Lois handed out glasses of champagne to the visitors. "On behalf of the spirits of Thornley house, I welcome you." I laid it on thick, wanting to make sure everyone got their money's worth. "Augustus Thornley purchased this beautiful home for his daughter, Norma."

At her cue, Jennifer glided down the stairway, stopping midway where everyone could see her. She was a vision from another time.

"These are the very stairs where Norma fell to her death."

The lights went out as a cold blast of air shot through the house. One of the women screamed before the lights flickered back to life.

"So sorry," I said. "Norma hates being reminded of the night she died."

The room erupted in chatter and conjecture. I loudly announced, "Please help yourself to appetizers. We'll start the tour of the rest of the house shortly."

The lights were my idea, activated by a remote control in my pocket, but the cold blast of air made it extra-creepy. I stepped into the kitchen to thank my ghost chef for helping with the spooky ambiance. "Emile?" I called out softly. "Where are you?"

A shiver ran up my arms as he appeared, a shimmery, transparent apparition.

"I have told you before, I am always here. Where else would I go?"

"How would I know?" My expertise included exotic teas and scrumptious pastries, not the afterlife. "I wanted to thank you for conjuring the gust of cold wind. Very impressive."

He gave me a bored look. "I am not a trained circus animal here to do tricks for you."

"Fine. Don't admit it." Perhaps Emile didn't want to disclose he enjoyed participating in the Halloween antics. Or perhaps Norma had finally decided to make her presence known in a more obvious way.

"Believe what you wish." With one more shimmer, he faded away completely.

I hurried back to my guests, prepared to give them a tour of the rest of the house.

The group nibbled canapés I'd made from Chef Emile's cookbook. I'd also made mummy hot dogs—basically pigs in blankets but cuter. Noises overhead told me someone had decided to investigate the second floor, not willing to wait for the tour to begin.

I made it halfway up the stairs before Bambi emerged at the top, out of breath, with flushed cheeks.

"I was looking for the ladies' room."

Sure, you were. I forced a smile. "The guest bathroom is on the first floor behind the stairs. I'll show you."

"I know where it is," she snipped. "That Crazy Cat Lady is occupying it. Old ladies take forever. I don't know what they do in there."

I asked Bambi, "Did you see anyone else upstairs?"

Instead of answering me, she pursed her blood-red lips in a pout. "Do you know where Joey is?"

"Joey?" I asked. "Your boyfriend in the doctor's costume?"

She stomped past me on the stairs. "He's not my boyfriend."

THE FIRST SIX NIGHTS OF THE HAUNTED HOUSE tour had gone off without a hitch, but this group behaved about as well as a bunch of unruly toddlers. As I attempted to corral the guests and begin the tour, a blood-curdling scream rang out from the floor above. I laughed that someone had discovered one of my handyman's scary props. Served them right for wandering off.

The witch, the warlock, Lois, and Bambi were in the front room along with Jennifer, so I went into the kitchen where I found Miss America reaching in the refrigerator for another bottle of champagne. It had been a woman's scream, so it must have been Crazy Cat Lady unless she was still in the restroom.

"Have you seen your friend?" I asked Miss America who was occupied peeling the foil off a bottle of Korbel.

"She can take care of herself," she said.

Some friend. "Stay here," I ordered. Before I could investigate further, loud steps clomped down the back set of stairs originally built for servants to use. Cat Lady appeared, ashen-faced and wide-eyed.

"There she is," Miss America said, stating the obvious.

Cat Lady clutched one of the stuffed cats pinned to her robe. "I- I saw a body."

I jumped at the pop from the champagne bottle.

Miss America poured two glasses and handed one to her friend. "This was supposed to be a haunted house tour, not a murder mystery party. We should have been told. She's got a weak heart."

"We're not staging a murder mystery." *Why would she take an old lady with a heart condition to a haunted house?* I turned to Cat Lady. "Where did you see this body?"

Between gulps of champagne, she said one word. "Kitchen."

"What are you talking about?" Miss America asked. "There's no corpse here."

"Not this kitchen. Upstairs."

"Will you show me?" I asked.

She shook her head violently. "I'm not going back up there." She guzzled the last of her drink, followed it up with a loud burp, and held her glass out for a refill.

I glanced at Chef who must have been

listening to us based on his amused expression. He'd never done anything so corporeal. He looked up from his saucepan and said, "You are sadly mistaken if you believe I'm interested in participating in your tomfoolery. I believe I made my position clear on that subject."

"Maybe Norma is joining in on the fun," I said to the group, without conviction. She made her presence known so rarely and always in subtle ways. Chef's scowl told me he didn't agree with my suggestion.

Cat Lady protested. "It was a real body." She pouted as if disappointed we weren't taking her seriously. "And besides, I don't believe in ghosts."

Before I could interrogate her further, Lois joined us. "What's going on? Doing a little extra for Halloween?"

"Not on purpose. One of the guests," I gestured at Cat Lady, "says she saw a dead body in the upstairs kitchen. I'm going to check."

Cat Lady grabbed my arm. "Don't go. The murderer might still be up there. You might be next."

"Murderer?" Lois said. "You think someone was murdered? If you're making this up just to freak everyone out—"

"I'm not," Cat Lady insisted. "There really is a dead body."

"There's only one way to find out," I said.

Lois stood in front of the stairs as if to stop me. "Let's call the police."

I smiled, hoping my calm voice would reassure her. "My handyman did some extra decorating for tonight. He probably got a hold of a mannequin or a CPR dummy and left it up there for effect. Wouldn't we look silly if we called the police over something like that?"

Lois stepped aside reluctantly, and I climbed the steps to the second floor.

I flipped on the lights in the upstairs kitchen. Relieved to find no body on the linoleum floor, I checked the rest of the rooms. The parlor held a sofa and coffee table but appeared otherwise empty... until I looked behind the door.

"What are you doing here?" I asked the fake doctor.

He pushed past me toward the stairs, taking them two at a time until he joined the others on the first floor.

I checked that my bedroom door remained locked and tried Jennifer's door, glad she'd remembered to lock hers for once. I took a quick look in the bathroom before returning to the kitchen. Still no body, thank goodness, but two half-full flutes sat on the counter. One of the glasses had a smudge the color of Bambi's lipstick on the rim. She must have been up here with someone. The fake doctor?

A stethoscope lay against the far wall. I picked up a crumpled piece of paper and flattened it out. The note, signed with the letter "A", read: *Meet me upstairs in five minutes.* Perhaps Bambi hadn't been in the room with the fake doctor after all. Had Andrew lured the nurse for some sort of groping session, and had Bambi's boyfriend followed them? But then why had he hidden in my parlor?

I returned to the first floor and found Lois. She took a quick count and said, "All of my guests are here. Have you seen Andrew?"

"He's not upstairs," I said. "I searched the whole floor."

We split up, looking for her assistant. I grabbed two flashlights, handing one to Lois, and we searched the backyard, including the garage. When we returned, I climbed the stairs again, this time planning to look in the attic.

As I opened the door to the attic, a skeleton dressed in a wig and tattered wedding gown swung toward me, a mournful wail filling the air. I screamed, then scolded myself for being so jumpy. I didn't expect to be the victim of one of my handyman's pranks.

Whisk, a sleek Bengal cat who refused to

come downstairs, sat on his favorite Windsor chair and gazed at me imperiously, undisturbed by thc commotion.

"Did you happen to see anyone come up here?" I asked him.

Whisk closed his eyes tightly then opened them, a gesture I took to mean no. Plenty of people talked to cats, though some people might think I was nuts interpreting his responses. Just in case, I took a quick look around, but nothing appeared out of place.

I returned to the second floor and found Jennifer waiting for me in the hall.

She wrung her hands nervously. "Did you find anything?"

"No. Maybe the cat lady is a prankster."

Jennifer's brows creased with concern. "I don't think saying you found a body is very funny."

I wholeheartedly agreed. "There's no accounting for some people's sense of humor. Let's go back downstairs and finish the tour if anyone is still interested."

"Is it okay if I change first? I spilled something on my dress." Jennifer reached for her door handle and seemed surprised when it didn't turn. "Did you lock my door?"

"No. You must have. I'll get the spare key from my room."

I returned and unlocked her door. She pushed it open but didn't enter. Her mouth dropped open, and her gaze locked on something inside.

"What is it?" I pushed past her into the room. On the floor lay Andrew, his unseeing eyes staring at the ceiling. I knelt beside him to check for a pulse but didn't feel even a flutter. Red marks encircled his neck.

"Is he…?" Jennifer didn't finish her question.

"Yes." I stared at his lifeless body, my heart breaking for a young life cut short. "He's dead."

Reminding myself to breathe, I dialed the number for Deputy Alex Molina, the acting Police Chief on loan from the sheriff's department. The county assigned us a single deputy for our town of 964 mostly law-abiding residents.

I left Jennifer in the hallway while I hurried downstairs, where I pulled Lois aside to tell her the tragic news. Her hand flew to her mouth as she gasped.

"Andrew? Dead?" Her voice quavered in disbelief. "But how?"

It would be best for her to hear the details from the authorities. "We'll know more soon, I hope."

I recruited Lois to keep everyone gathered in the main room and returned to Jennifer. She didn't like being so close to Andrew's body, so I took over the task of hall monitor and sent her downstairs to make a few pots of tea for our guests.

The doorbell rang, and moments later heavy footsteps pounded up the stairs. Deputy Molina didn't look a day over thirty with his dark, unruly hair and baby face. "Where's the victim?"

I pointed at Jennifer's door, letting him see for himself. "Is Dr. Severs coming?"

"She's on her way."

We didn't have long to wait. Dr. Fredeline Severs, our local doctor and county coroner, had befriended me when I moved to town. She climbed the stairs wearing a spaghetti-strap dress, her dark skin glowing and her hair in perfect spiral curls.

"Hi Freddie, um, Dr. Severs." I pointed her toward Jennifer's room. "Sorry you had to cut your evening short," I said, guessing she'd been on a date.

She shrugged. "I'm used to it." She greeted

Molina as he emerged from the room. "What do we have?"

"According to the woman downstairs, his name is Andrew Laughton," Molina said. "He appears to be the victim of strangulation."

I'd figured as much from marks on his neck. "What was he strangled with?"

Molina scowled at me, then addressed Dr. Severs. "I didn't see anything in the room that appeared to be a likely murder weapon, but I haven't had a chance to do a thorough search."

Since he'd been newly assigned to our town, I didn't want him to think I was challenging his authority. "Of course." I turned to Freddie and added, "He just got here."

"Got it," she said. "I'll examine Andrew now if it's all right with you two."

"Deputy." I waved him out into the hallway. "Can I show you something?"

He followed me to the kitchen, and I showed him what I'd found. "The note was lying on the floor. I had no idea there had been a murder, otherwise, I wouldn't have touched it with my bare hands. But I didn't touch the stethoscope. Do you think it could have been the murder weapon?"

"It's possible." He picked it up with a gloved hand for a closer look. "I'll ask Dr. Severs. She should be able to compare it with the ligature marks on the victim's neck to confirm. Also, strangulation can leave DNA on the object used."

After bagging the stethoscope, he read the note. "You think Andrew wrote this note? But who was he meeting?"

"I bet it was Bambi if that's even her real name. I caught her upstairs—she claimed she was looking for the ladies' room. That was twenty or thirty minutes before Cat Lady screamed. And if I'm not mistaken, the lipstick on one of those champagne flutes matches Bambi's."

"Wait. Back up," he said, raising his eyebrows. "Cat Lady?"

"One of the older ladies is dressed as a crazy cat lady. She screamed when she found the body here in the kitchen, but it was several minutes before I came upstairs. The killer must have hidden the body in Jennifer's room, engaging the lock before he closed it, hoping we wouldn't look there right away."

Molina motioned for me to step into the hallway, then put crime scene tape over the kitchen doorway.

I continued with my theory. "What if the so-called doctor followed them up here and strangled Andrew in a jealous rage? I found him in the upstairs parlor when I came upstairs to look for the body."

"So, you think he murdered the victim, moved his body into the bedroom, and then just relaxed in your parlor waiting to be discovered?" His voice oozed incredulity.

"He was hiding behind the door. It's possible he didn't have a chance to come downstairs without being seen."

"I'm in charge here, and I'll do the investigation," he said, in a scolding tone. "If you'll wait with the others, I'll be down to question everyone shortly, including you."

As I slowly made my way down the staircase, I pondered the evening's events. After strangling Andrew in the kitchen, the killer must have hidden when he heard Cat Lady's footsteps. When she screamed and ran downstairs, he carried or dragged the body to Jennifer's room to hide it.

The only person unaccounted for at the time? The fake doctor.

But why move the body? He might have intended to remove all the evidence from the kitchen and been interrupted. If Cat Lady hadn't screamed, and if Jennifer hadn't decided to change out of her gown, we might not have discovered Andrew's body until everyone else had left.

A slender, boyish-looking uniformed officer stood by the front door. Either it was a costumed latecomer to the tour, or Molina had recruited another officer to assist him. I assumed the latter, but I doubted this young deputy had the experience to contribute much to the investigation.

Molina would need help solving this murder, whether he wanted it or not. While he wasn't likely to listen to my theories, Freddie was smart, experienced, and intuitive. She'd listen to me.

I'd make sure of it.

JENNIFER AND I PLACED POTS OF DARJEELING, chamomile, and peppermint tea on the tables along with cups, saucers, milk, and sugar.

Earlier that day, I'd made individual servings of a dessert known as Death by Chocolate. As Jennifer set the glass cups filled with chocolate and cream layers on a tray, I leaned close and whispered, "If anyone asks, it's called Chocolate Delight."

I prepared another tray with homemade shortbread cookies, and we took the desserts to the tearoom and began serving. The group began to relax as they ate, drank, and exchanged rumors about what might have happened to Andrew.

Deputy Molina came downstairs, a somber look on his face. Once he'd made sure Lois and her tour guests were all present and accounted for, he stood at the front of the room and addressed them.

"As you may be aware, there was a sad occurrence here this evening. Andrew Laughton has died under possibly suspicious circumstances."

Possibly?

"If I may impose on you a little longer," he continued, "I'll need to question each of you individually. I'll make it as quick as I can, but everyone must stay until I've completed my interviews." He walked over to Cat Lady. "I'd like you to come with me, please."

Molina asked me which room would afford the most privacy, and I directed him to a room I called the library, a former bedroom now used for private events. He ushered Cat Lady inside and closed the door.

I took a seat by the fire and waved Jennifer over. Freddie came downstairs and headed toward us. I offered her a glass of champagne, but she declined since her workday was far from over. She sat down and stared into the fire.

"Pretty cut and dry, isn't it?" I asked.

"Uh-huh." Her attention seemed to be focused elsewhere, no doubt on the dead body upstairs.

"Was the stethoscope the murder weapon?" I asked.

She raised her eyebrows. "Did Molina tell you about that?"

"I saw it in the kitchen where Cat Lady found the body."

She nodded. "The ligature marks are consistent with the stethoscope, but please keep it to yourselves. If we can retrieve DNA that matches the victim, that will confirm it's the murder weapon."

"That settles it, then," Jennifer said. "It was Joey's stethoscope. He's the murderer."

"That's completely circumstantial," Freddie said. "Not that people haven't been convicted of crimes on purely circumstantial evidence, mind you." She leaned back in her chair, tapping her fingers against her leg, again deep in thought.

Jennifer looked from me to Freddie and back to me. "Okay, if it's not Joey, it has to be one of the others."

"Yep," I agreed. "One of the six is a murderer." I counted them off on my fingers. "Joey, Bambi, the witch, the warlock, Crazy Cat Lady, or Miss America."

"Seven," Freddie said, lowering her voice. "You're forgetting Lois."

"It can't be Lois," Jennifer said, her voice barely more than a whisper. "Can it?"

"Everyone's a suspect until Molina confirms their whereabouts at the time of the murder," Freddie said. "Even you two."

Jennifer frowned. "Us?"

"Don't worry," I said to reassure her. "I'm sure you have an alibi for the time of death."

"Which was when, exactly?" Freddie asked.

I stared at her. "Good question." I turned to Jennifer. "I don't remember seeing Andrew after they first arrived."

"Me either." Jennifer thought for a moment. "So, the time of the murder had to have been sometime between when everyone arrived and when Cat Lady screamed."

"Bambi would know better," I said.

"Bambi?" Freddie asked. "The woman in the nurse's costume?"

"Yes. I think she met Andrew in the upstairs kitchen before he was murdered. I'm guessing Joey followed them up there."

"April May?" Deputy Molina's booming voice startled me. "May I have a word?"

I stood and followed the deputy into the library. The wood-paneled room, lined with bookshelves had a cozy feel. I never expected it would be used for interviewing murder suspects.

We sat across from each other in two leather wing-back chairs, a round mahogany table between us. I dove right into my theory.

"I'm thinking Andrew made a pass at Bambi, and her boyfriend Joey, the fake doctor, followed them upstairs to confront them."

Molina leaned back in his chair. "Go on."

"They must have fought, and Joey strangled him." It seemed the obvious conclusion.

"That must have made quite a commotion," he said.

I searched my memory. "I heard footsteps when Bambi went upstairs earlier. But she doesn't look strong enough to strangle a man. And she'd come downstairs before Cat Lady screamed, so she couldn't have moved the body."

His eyebrows drew together in concentration. "Dr. Severs and I didn't find any evidence that the body had been moved."

"That doesn't make sense. Then why did Cat Lady –"

Molina held up a hand to stop me. "I'm interested in the facts, not your theories. This case will be solved by diligent and orderly processing of the evidence. What I need from you is information to construct an accurate timeline of the evening complete with everyone's movements."

"That's a great idea. We can start with—"

He held up his hand again, which was starting to annoy me. "We'll start with the arrival of Lois, Andrew, and the six tour guests."

"Of course." I proceeded to provide him with the details of the evening's events as I remembered them, ending with Molina's arrival.

He took copious notes. Expecting to be complimented for my keen observation skills and precise memory, I found myself disappointed by his lack of appreciation.

He stood. "That will be all for now."

MY STOMACH GRUMBLED, AND I DUCKED INTO THE kitchen for a snack, having forgotten to eat anything in the excitement.

Chef Emile leaned against the far counter, a glass of wine in his hand. As soon as everyone left, I'd be pouring a big glass for myself.

"Did you hear we found a body in Jennifer's bedroom?" I asked.

"It would be impossible not to be aware, with the incessant prattling of strangers as they traipse in and out of my kitchen." He sighed as if feeling put upon by the mortal guests.

"Did you happen to see anything unusual? Like someone sneaking through the kitchen and up the back stairs?"

"Why yes," Chef said, a smile playing on his lips. "An entire family has been creeping about. Did you not see them?"

I sighed. Getting a straight answer from the Chef about anything that didn't involve cooking techniques was futile.

I grabbed a plate of cheese puffs and left the kitchen to join the others. Lois had joined Jennifer by the fire.

Jennifer spoke in a hushed tone. "Bambi was in the living room with us when Cat Lady screamed, so she couldn't have moved the body." She paused. "What about the witch and warlock? They might have done it together."

Lois shook her head. "They stayed in the tearoom drinking champagne and eating appetizers from the time we arrived until..." She left the words unsaid. Her tight-lipped smile told me her emotions were barely in check. "I'm their alibi, and they're mine, in case you forgot I'm a suspect, too."

I hadn't forgotten, but I was glad to cross her off my list. "I'm sorry about Andrew."

She stared at the ground and shook her head. "I didn't know him well—just hired him a few weeks ago for the tours. Seemed like a nice kid. Polite." She took a deep breath and let out a sigh. "I guess you're getting old when you call twenty-five-year-old men kids."

Molina asked to talk with Lois next. Miss America emerged from the kitchen managing her walker and a bottle of champagne. I turned in my chair to check on the other guests.

"It's one of you," the woman in the witch costume said, waving a finger at the others. "One of you is a murderer."

Miss America handed her the bottle. "Shut up and pour yourself another drink. We might be here for a while."

The group seemed smaller than it should have been. I counted the guests. Five plus Lois.

I walked over to Bambi. "Where's Cat Lady?"

"How should I know? Probably in the little girls' room again."

Before I could check the restroom, an ambulance arrived. Dr. Severs conferred with the attendants to arrange transport of the body to the county morgue. The two men went upstairs, and Freddie followed to supervise.

Molina and Lois emerged, and the deputy motioned for Joey to follow him to the library. I found Jennifer in the kitchen eating a Chocolate Delight.

She gave me a guilty look. "It's my second one."

"Chocolate always helps cheer me up. Besides, it has antioxidants and flavanols. Lots of health benefits," I concluded as the door swung open.

Freddie appeared. "In that case, I'll take one of those, too."

I handed her a dessert. "Molina doesn't think the body was moved. Do you think he's right?"

"It's possible," Freddie said.

Jennifer's eyes widened. "You think he was killed in my room?" She turned to me. "Can I move into the other bedroom? Like tonight?"

I patted her shoulder to reassure her. "Of course."

"There's no sign of a struggle in either room," Freddie said, "so it's likely he was killed quickly, perhaps taken by surprise."

"But what about the body that Cat Lady saw?" Jennifer asked.

What about the body? "Maybe she just stumbled over something in the dark." But there hadn't been anything in the room except the glasses, the stethoscope, and the note. Three obvious and convenient clues pointing to Joey as the killer.

The realization hit me. "There never was a body. At least not where Cat Lady said it was."

"So, Cat Lady lied?" Jennifer asked, looking more confused than before.

"Are you thinking what I'm thinking?" I asked Freddie.

Her eyes fixed on mine as if trying to read my mind. "If you are referring to the clues that were tied up neatly with a bow and served to us on a platter, then yes."

"That is exactly what I'm thinking," I said, glad we agreed. "Did you say anything to the deputy?"

"He said sometimes criminals are stupid and leave enough evidence to hang themselves."

"Wait," Jennifer said, clearly confused. "Why would Cat Lady lie about finding a body? And how could she have known there was a dead body if she didn't find it?"

"Only one way." I lowered my voice. "She's the murderer."

Jennifer gasped. "That old lady?"

"Shh," I motioned for her to be quiet, not sure how well our voices carried into the other room. "I'm betting she's not as old as she's pretending to be. I knew there was something off about her. Think about it. You put on a gray wig and glasses, wear a baggy robe, hunch over, and move slowly, and no one looks closer to see how many wrinkles you have."

Freddie and Jennifer followed me into the tearoom just as Molina and Joey emerged from the library, Joey with his hands cuffed behind him.

"I'm telling you," Joey moaned. "I didn't kill anyone."

"Sure," Molina grumbled. "That's why you were hiding behind a door in one of the upstairs rooms."

"I told you," Joey said, frustration in his voice. "Bambi told me to meet her up there."

I waved the deputy over frantically, and he gave me a perturbed frown. He took Joey by the elbow and led him to us.

"He might be right," I said. "I don't think he killed Andrew."

Joey's face brightened with hope.

Molina glared at me. "Don't interfere with my investigation. I've arrested Mr. Barlowe and I'm taking him in." He turned to Freddie, perhaps seeking support, but it was his turn to be disappointed.

"I agree with April." She lowered her voice to just above a whisper. "I think Cat Lady killed Andrew."

"Uh, oh." I looked around the room, a bad feeling in my bones.

Freddie asked, "What is it?"

"Bambi said Cat Lady was in the restroom. Either she has major gastrointestinal issues..."

Freddie completed the sentence. "Or she's gone."

Molina handcuffed Joey to a chair in front of the fireplace and headed toward the others. "Where's Charlotte Lucas?" he demanded. When no one responded, he said, "The Crazy Cat Lady."

With no answer from the group, he enlisted Freddie, Jennifer, and me to help him search the premises. I took the attic, happy that nothing jumped out at me this time.

"Whisk?" I called out. I heard a noise and found the cat in a box full of old framed photos. "That can't be comfortable."

He gave me a look that clearly said, "Go away and quit bothering me," but one of the pictures caught my eye.

In shades of sepia, it showed three generations of women in long dresses. I guessed by the clothing style that it had been taken more than a hundred years earlier. Funny how some features persisted from generation to generation. These three women, who at first glance looked very different from each other, were obviously related, with the same high cheekbones and prominent chin.

Chef's words popped into my head. *An entire family has been creeping about.*

I dropped the photo and rushed down both sets of stairs to the main floor. One look at Bambi and Miss America confirmed my suspicions. With their significant age difference, they bore little resemblance to each other, except for a distinctive cleft chin.

I hurried over to Molina, who held his notes in one hand with his phone up to his ear.

He brightened when a voice came on the other end of the line. "May I speak with Charlotte Lucas?"

His body appeared to deflate as he listened to the response. He ended the phone call.

"What's wrong?" I asked the deputy, as Jennifer approached us.

"She gave me a wrong number."

"It's a phony name," Jennifer said. "Charlotte Lucas is a character from *Pride and Prejudice*."

"How was I supposed to know that?" Molina whined. He ignored my attempt to get his attention, and instead walked over to the table where the other guests waited. When he returned, his expression was glum. "The woman she arrived with claims they just met tonight, and she doesn't know her name or number."

He dropped into a chair in front of the fire and put his head in his hands. "I really screwed up this time. So much for getting promoted. I'll be lucky if I'm able to keep my job after this debacle."

"I have some information for you." When he looked up, I said, "I'm pretty sure Bambi and Miss America are related—probably grandmother and granddaughter."

He pulled his eyebrows together as he tried to understand the significance of what I was saying. "What does that have to do with Charlotte?" He gestured with air quotes when he said Cat Lady's fake name.

"They both have a cleft chin, and if I remember correctly, so did Cat Lady. I think the three of them are related and planned the murder together."

Molina gave me a hopeful look. "You think so?"

"Someone must have lured Andrew upstairs, don't you think?" It made sense to me. I also had a good idea who did the luring.

"Bambi?" Molina guessed.

I nodded. "Is that her real name?"

"Yes, according to her driver's license. You think she's in on it?"

"She was upstairs right around the time of the murder."

"What about the old lady?" Molina asked. "What did she have to do with it?"

I shrugged. "Maybe she was a sort of lookout to make sure the plan went smoothly. And it did until Jennifer opened her bedroom door. How would you ever have solved the case if everyone had left before Andrew's body had been found?"

"It would have been nearly impossible," he admitted.

Molina asked Bambi and Miss America to come with him. He cuffed the older woman to a chair next to Joey and asked Freddie to keep an eye on both while he questioned Bambi.

He returned, a peeved expression on his face.

I followed him as he escorted Miss America to the library. "What did you get out of Bambi?" I whispered.

"Wait in there," Molina said to Miss America. He closed the door behind her. "I got nothing out of Bambi," he told me. "She claims she's never met any of these people before tonight besides Joey and said she doesn't even know him well." He glanced back at her, and I followed his gaze.

She sat stoic, her lips tight as if sealing the truth from us.

"But here's something interesting." He lowered his voice. "When I talked to Joey earlier, he said he knew Andrew. They used to work together selling retirement investments. Joey claims he got out of it when he realized what a scam it was, but I think he lost his job when the company folded."

"So, you think Bambi might be lying about not knowing Andrew?" I asked.

He shrugged. "I don't know what to think at this point." He glanced over where Freddie and Bambi sat. "Maybe she'll open up to the two of you." He looked me square in the eye. "And if not, maybe she'll talk once she realizes the gravity of the situation. I'm going to question Miss America now and come back to Bambi after I see what I learn."

"Good luck."

Jennifer and I rejoined Freddie and Bambi by the fire. I kept my eyes on Bambi while I talked. I addressed my two friends but made sure Bambi overheard. "They must have had a good reason for wanting Andrew dead."

"Like what?" Jennifer asked. "What could be worth killing someone over?"

"I don't know. Maybe Andrew hurt someone they cared about." I watched Bambi's expression.

No reaction.

"Or stole something really valuable." I'd just keep guessing until I struck a nerve. "Maybe he talked her into one of those sketchy retirement investments." I could have sworn that Bambi flinched. "Is that what happened?"

Bambi narrowed her eyes but said nothing.

"Too bad you and Miss America are going to have to go to jail because you won't tell the deputy the truth."

Her eyes widened, and I sensed that I was on the right track. I kept poking. "It's tough for anyone to be locked up, but at her age, it's going to be a traumatic experience."

Freddie joined in. "The other inmates don't always respect their elders. The prison guards can be brutal, and they treat every criminal the same."

"What do I care?" Bambi bluffed. "I don't even know her."

"Great. Then it won't bother you to think of her lying on a hard bed in a jail cell because of you and your mother."

"How did you know—?" She stopped, no doubt realizing she'd said too much.

"Just an educated guess," I said. "Thanks for

confirming it. Why did you do it, Bambi? Why did you lure Andrew upstairs so that your mother could strangle him?"

Her face contorted as she attempted to maintain control over her emotions. A tear ran down her cheek, followed by another. "I can't—" she sobbed. "I won't—"

I spoke gently, hoping to get her to see reason. "Talk to Molina. You can make a deal to keep her out of jail."

She shook her head. "My family is all I have. I won't betray them."

"You don't have a choice," Freddie said. "Betray your mother or betray your grandmother."

Bambi wiped her nose with the back of her hand. For now, she was done talking.

Molina led Bambi and Miss America toward the front door, Bambi in handcuffs and Miss America pushing her walker.

"Wait," Bambi said. "I can't do this, Grandma."

"Bambi, no," the older woman said. "Your mother did it for me." She grabbed Bambi's arm. "Don't say anything."

"Did she do it for you?" Bambi asked, her voice rising. "Did you get any of your money back? That's what she told me this was all about. And where is she? She left us to take the fall." She laughed ruefully. "At least Mom made sure you'll have a roof over your head. In prison."

"They've got nothing on us, sweetie," Bambi's grandmother said, dismissing her with a wave of her hand. "They'll keep us overnight and let us go."

Molina cleared his throat. "The D.A. will charge both of you with accessory to murder, carrying up to fifteen years in prison. Is that what you want for your grandmother?"

The older woman scoffed. "He's bluffing."

Molina ignored her and focused on Bambi. "She could die in jail. If you don't tell us now how to find your mother, and she gets away, it will be much worse for both of you."

"She's—" Bambi began. She glanced at her grandmother then stared at the floor. "She's at the airport," she mumbled, breaking down in tears.

Once Molina got Bambi's mother's true name and an accurate description of the 43-year-old woman, he put out an APB. He then escorted Bambi and her grandmother to the police station.

Lois clapped her hands and announced to the few remaining guests, "The remainder of tonight's tour is canceled. Please contact the office in the morning if you would like a refund."

I heard a voice say, "I think we got our money's worth."

Lois led her group out the front door, and I waved goodbye before retrieving the last champagne bottle from the refrigerator and filling two flutes. Once I'd returned to my spot in front of the fire, I handed one to Jennifer.

"Wow. What an awful night. And what awful people." Jennifer took a long sip of her drink. "The only thing I don't understand is why did they try to frame Joey? I mean, they might have gotten away with it if they hadn't concocted such a complicated plan, don't you think?"

I leaned back in my chair, exhausted from the night's events. "Deputy Molina said Joey knew Andrew, so maybe he was involved in the retirement scam. I'd guess that Andrew sold Bambi's grandmother on the scheme, but Joey was involved somehow. Cat Lady figured she could kill two birds with one stone. Or rather, kill one bird and send the other to prison for murder."

"Next Halloween," Jennifer said with a half-grin, "Let's skip the haunted house tour and spend the evening doing something boring. Forget about these stupid ghosts."

A cold wind swept through the house and the lights flickered off.

"That's not funny," Jennifer said, her voice shaky.

"I didn't do it on purpose. I must have bumped the remote." I reached in my pockets, but they were empty. "Where did the remote go?" Goosebumps ran up my arms as the lights flashed back on.

Jennifer and I locked eyes. "Norma!"

MUMMY HOT DOGS

AKA SPOOKY PIGS IN A BLANKET

INGREDIENTS:

- 1 tube (8 oz.) refrigerated crescent rolls
- 1 (14 oz.) package mini hot dogs
- 1 large egg
- 1 Tablespoon yellow mustard

DIRECTIONS:

1. Preheat oven to 375 F (190 C)
2. Roll out the crescent roll dough to make one big sheet, pressing the seams together. Cut into thin strips.

3. Wrap a strip of dough around each hot dog, stretching to make them look like bandages. Leave a space exposed on the top for the face.
4. Set mummy dogs on ungreased baking sheet spaced slightly apart. Whisk the egg and brush some of the egg wash on the dough.
5. Bake 10-12 minutes until light to medium brown. Use a toothpick and some mustard to make eyes.

TEA IS FOR TRADITION

A HAUNTED TEAROOM THANKSGIVING STORY

PRESENT TIME

APRIL

The ghost of Chef Emile Toussaint watched as I prepared our Thanksgiving Feast. I'd made a sweet potato casserole the day before and got up early so that the huge, 22-pound turkey would be ready when everyone arrived that afternoon. I had Chef's cookbook, *Modern French Cooking,* propped open to his recipe for Spinach au Gratin.

"What was Thanksgiving like when you were..." I didn't want to say, 'when you were alive,' so I said, "when you were head chef here?" My Victorian home had housed a French restaurant in the nineteen fifties and sixties. That was one of the reasons I'd decided it would be perfect for my tearoom, since much of the work required for a restaurant had already been done.

"Ah, *ma chérie*, the delicacies I created lured diners from all over the state. The champagne, it flowed like water. Of course, I did not partake until after the meal was served."

"Of course not." I knew how much Chef loved his wine. "Not even one glass?"

The corners of his mouth twitched. "Perhaps, but only one."

A quick rap on the back door told me my neighbor Irma had arrived to help prepare our feast. When she entered the kitchen, she took off her coat and hat and patted down her short gray hair in a futile attempt to tame it.

"Irma was around back then, you know," I said to Chef. "She can tell me what really happened."

Irma leaned her walking stick against the counter and set a bag on the kitchen island. "I was where?"

"At Thanksgiving when Norma first opened the restaurant here." Norma and her sister Barbara were the previous owners of what was now my home.

"I was just a kid back then. It was around 1955 or '56 when Barbara got married and moved out. I heard she wanted her sister to sell the house so they could split the money, but Norma had other ideas."

Irma had told me when I first arrived in town that Norma took out most of the walls on the main floor and turned it into a French restaurant, Maison Rose. She lured Emile from a restaurant in Beverly Hills and promised him she would help him publish his cookbooks, which she did. I owned copies of all three of them.

"Chef was just telling me about the Thanksgiving dinners he prepared back then. When I was growing up, our Thanksgiving meal was a dried out, overcooked turkey, instant mashed potatoes, and canned green beans. I usually filled up on the sweet potato casserole with the marshmallows on top. And crescent rolls baked from a tube, of course."

"No wonder you learned how to cook."

I chuckled. "I was fourteen years old the first time I attempted Thanksgiving dinner. My mother never was much of a cook, so she was more than happy to turn over the reins to me. My brother complained about my homemade cranberry sauce. He wanted the canned kind."

Irma shrugged. "It's kind of mandatory, don't you think?"

My assistant Jennifer came clomping down the back staircase. "Oh, good. Irma's here. Did you bring the recipe for the cranberry pretzel Jell-O salad?"

Irma patted the bag she'd brought. "Sure did."

"The what?" I asked, thinking I must have heard wrong. "If you're putting Jell-O and pretzels in a salad, thanks but no thanks."

"Aw, c'mon. At least give it a try. My mom made it every Thanksgiving, and I haven't had it since, well, you know." Jennifer's mother had passed away a few years earlier, and her grief was still close to the surface.

My heart did a little flip and I tried to backpedal as quickly as possible. "Then we should totally make it. I insist."

"And you'll try it?" Jennifer gave me puppy dog eyes.

"You bet. I can't wait. Do you have all the ingredients?"

Irma pointed to the bag she'd set on the island. "Everything's in there. Want me to put it together?"

Jennifer grinned. "That would be great. I'm afraid I'll mess it up. Maybe there's something easy I can help with."

"You're so good at chopping, and there's plenty of that, especially when it comes to Chef's cornbread dressing." I handed her the cutting board along with several stalks of celery, two onions, and some garlic cloves. "That should keep you busy for a while."

"I'll start the Jell-O." Irma pulled a ceramic bowl from the cupboard and set the kettle on to boil. "Did Chef tell you about the Thanksgiving when Norma invited a bunch of VIPs to the restaurant?"

"Did she actually make you work on Thanksgiving?" From what I'd heard about Norma, that wouldn't surprise me.

"The event was the Sunday before. And when I say event, I mean it. She went all out, with French champagne and caviar. She invited a famous actor, although I didn't know who he was at the time and three restaurant critics from major publications. One of them actually showed up." Irma shook her head. "That woman could get people to do almost anything."

"Ah yes," Chef said, although I was the one who could hear him. "She had a certain *je ne sais quois*."

I repeated what he'd said to the others.

"*Je ne sais quois* means 'I don't know what,' right?" Irma scowled. "I know exactly what she had. She was narcissistic, manipulative, and—"

Before she could finish her sentence, the back door slammed open, and a cold gust of air swept through the room.

I put my hands on my hips in mock irritation and went to close the door. "I've warned you about saying unflattering things about Norma when you're in this house, but do you listen to me?" I'd never seen Norma's ghost, but I had felt her presence several times. "One of these days she's going to blow a fuse. And I mean that literally."

"I don't know how I'm going to tell the story without saying anything negative about Norma, but I can try."

Jennifer stopped chopping. "Story?"

"What story?" I asked.

"The story about one Thanksgiving dinner which nearly resulted in the restaurant closing its doors just three years after it opened. I'd just turned sixteen…"

1961

IRMA

I'd walked past Thornley House many times, hoping that when I got old enough, I could get a job working with Chef Emile Tousssaint, the Frenchman who Norma Thornley had lured to come and run the kitchen at her new restaurant, Maison Rose, three years earlier.

I'd always loved to cook, but never had any training, so the day I turned sixteen, I put on my best clothes and went to ask Miss Thornley for a job. I stood across the street staring at the Victo rian house for at least an hour trying to get up the nerve before I chickened out and walked back home. Who did I think I was, a teenager from Puerto Rico whose cooking skills pretty much began and ended with *Arroz con Pollo*?

Three days later I finally got up the nerve to knock on the front door. When the door swung open, Norma's sister Barbara stood staring at me. She resembled her sister superficially, though her dark hair was pulled back in a severe bun, and she had none of Norma's elegance. She'd moved out of the house she half-owned several years earlier when she'd married.

She scowled at me. "What do you want?"

"Is Miss Thornley in?"

She set her lips in a tight line, and I silently waited to see what she'd do. Finally, she closed the door again, leaving me standing on the porch.

A few minutes later, the door opened again and Norma Thornley appeared looking even more hoity-toity up close than she did from far away. My mouth went dry.

I blurted out, "I'd like a job in your kitchen, please."

Norma looked me up and down. "You're that Vargas girl, aren't you?"

"Yes, ma'am."

"Don't call me ma'am. I'm not all that much older than you. Which is… what?"

"I'm sixteen, ma'am." I swallowed hard. "Sorry, miss."

She looked me up and down. "I suppose that's

old enough to bus tables and take out the trash. Go around the back and if Emile wants to hire you, I won't object."

"Thank you, ma'am--miss!" I ran off around the side of the house before she could change her mind.

Out of breath, I banged on the back door, and moments later it swung open. A skinny boy not much older than me with more freckles than I'd ever seen on one person stared at me. His chef's hat was held up by his prominent ears.

"I'd like to see Chef Emile Toussaint, please," I told the boy. My nervousness turned into irritation when he kept staring at me and didn't say anything. "Did you hear me? Is Chef Emile here?"

He scurried back inside, leaving the door open so I could hear him talking. Then a voice with a heavy French accent spoke.

"What does this person want, Marty?"

"Um," the boy stammered. "I don't know."

Emile appeared, towering over me like a vision from a movie—silver-haired, handsome, and scowling. His chef's hat made him appear even taller. "Yes, what is it? Who are you?"

I stretched my neck trying to appear taller than my five feet zero inches. "I'm Irma Vargas and I'd like a job. Norma told me to speak with you."

"To work in the kitchen?" He narrowed his eyes. "But you are a girl."

"Yes, I know that. I can work as hard as any man. If you give me a chance, I promise you won't regret it. I want to learn to cook like you do."

Something about what I'd said struck him as funny. "Ah, such big words for such a *petite jeune fille*. Do you have any idea how hard the work is? Long hours standing on your feet—you would not last a week. No, I change my mind. You would not last a day."

I put my hands on my hips, determined not to take no for an answer. "Try me."

He stared at me for a long time before nodding. "You are very lucky it is hard to find workers in the middle of nowhere as we find ourselves." He paused, as if deciding. "Very well. I will try you. Wait here." A minute later, he returned with a white folded shirt, pants, and a hat. "These are the smallest I have. See what you can do with them and be back here tomorrow at noon."

"Yes, sir. Thank you, sir."

He frowned and crossed his arms, staring down at me. "You will give to me the respect that I deserve. In this kitchen, you do as you are told, and you address me in one way and one way only: Chef."

"Yes, Chef. Thank you, Chef, you won't regret it." I hurried home before he could change his mind.

CHEF WAS RIGHT ABOUT THE HARD WORK AND SORE feet. The first couple of nights I nearly cried myself to sleep from pain and exhaustion, but it got better. As the newest person on the staff, it was my job to clean up after everyone, carry out trash, and keep the floor spic and span. The moment anything dropped, I was to pick it up immediately so no one would slip and fall. While I worked, I watched and listened as Chef barked orders to the others.

Marty, the teenager with the big ears, cringed whenever Chef yelled at him. He reminded me of a stray puppy, so I would make faces at him to try to make him laugh. I never succeeded, probably because he was afraid it would incur Chef's wrath, but occasionally he would crack a smile.

One time, I returned from taking the rubbish out and found Chef screaming at Marty. "Where did you get these herbs?"

Marty cowered as he croaked his response. "From the garden."

"This." Chef held up few green sprigs. "This is parsley." He set it down and picked up a few others. "This is hemlock. Have you perhaps heard of hemlock?"

Marty squeaked a response that might have been yes or no.

"It is *poison.*" He said the word with a French accent—pwah-son. "Do you understand this word?"

"Poison?" Marty whispered.

"*Mais oui*! Show me where you have found this herb in my garden."

Chef followed Marty outside, and when they returned, Chef said little else the rest of the day. I meant to ask Marty what had happened, but the incident was soon forgotten.

I often stole carrots from Marty when he was chopping them. When he nicked his finger, not for the first time, Chef blew up and said several words in French. The only ones I recognized were, "*Sacré bleu!*"

He grabbed me by my arm and pulled me aside. "*Ma petite carotte,* what am I to do? Marty cannot do his work with you in the kitchen. One of you must go."

"But Chef," I protested. "I'll stop bothering him. I will—I promise."

He shook his head. "Ah, *ma chérie,* it is not so simple. He is, how you say? Smitten. And who can blame him, no? If I were twenty years younger, my head it would be turned, I am sure."

"But I love this job." I blinked back tears. "I want to learn to be a great Chef like you."

"Then it seems I must fire Marty." He sighed dramatically. "His mother will be very sad. She is a widow, you know."

I hung my head. Was Chef really going to make me responsible for what happened to Marty and his family?

Without warning, he snapped his fingers and said something in French, adding in English, "Come with me."

For the first time ever, I followed Chef into the dining room. I tiptoed through the elegantly decorated room marveling at the flocked wallpaper, polished mahogany furniture, and beautiful light sconces. I felt underdressed even though we were the only ones in the room.

"Wait here," he said as he reached the staircase.

At that moment, a vision in red descended from the upper floor. Norma Thornley wore an elegant off-the-shoulder gown with a skirt trimmed in ostrich feathers dyed to match.

"Mademoiselle Norma, I need to talk to you about this young woman." He gestured to me, and I forced a smile, still hopeful I could keep my job.

Norma looked down her nose at me. "What about her."

Chef took a few more steps until they were on the same level and whispered in her ear. They seemed so intimate with each other that I looked away.

After a few whispers back and forth, I heard Norma say, "It's simply not possible, Chef. Look at her!"

"She does not look like much dressed this way, I must admit." Chef came down the stairs, returned to my side, and snatched off my hat. "But see the cheekbones?" He grabbed my jaw and gently moved my head from side to side. "There is a bit of the Audrey Hepburn about her, *non*? Imagine her with *une nouvelle coiffure,* some rouge, and, well, something else to wear, naturally."

"Naturally," Norma said, a smile playing on her lips. She glided down the steps and came over to inspect me like I was a pork chop in the meat case. Finally, she gave us her conclusion. "I suppose I can see what I can do."

"Bon." Chef brushed his hands together in a swift motion. "I shall leave her in your hands."

I watched Chef return to the kitchen without me and turned to Norma to learn my fate.

"Congratulations," she said. "You're our new hostess. Let's make you look presentable, shall we?"

I WOULD COME TO WORK IN MY OWN CLOTHES AND when I arrived at Thornley House, Norma would hand me a dress to wear. She instructed me on how to style my hair and what cosmetics to purchase with my meager earnings.

One evening as I gave her back the dress I'd worn that day, she waved me away. "Oh, just keep it. Heaven knows, I'll never wear it again." She added a warning. "But don't you dare put that in a wringer washer."

Over the next few weeks, she gave me nearly a dozen couture dresses from Dior, Chanel, Balenciaga, and others as well. They were from previous years' collections, which meant she wouldn't allow herself to be seen in public in them.

I thought they were divine. My mother, an expert seamstress, helped me take them in using hand stitches so we didn't make any permanent changes. Norma could be volatile, and I worried that one day she'd change her mind and ask for all the dresses back.

On the Sunday before Thanksgiving, I arrived four hours earlier than usual as she had instructed. Norma had invited several VIP guests for an early Thanksgiving feast and wanted everything to be absolutely perfect.

She handed me a pair of rubber gloves and set me to scrubbing every inch of the dining room. Once that task was completed to her satisfaction, she sent me to ask Chef if he needed my help. I saw this as my chance to find out who exactly was coming to dinner.

Chef raised an eyebrow when I entered the kitchen. "What are you doing in my kitchen?" he said in a teasing tone. "Only kitchen staff is allowed in here."

"Norma sent me to ask if you needed anything."

"Is that so? You may inform her I have everything under control, *comme d'habitude*."

"*Mais bien sûr*," I said, using one of the few French phrases I'd learned. I paused, then bravely launched into my question. "What's the big deal about tonight, Chef? Who's coming to dinner? I've never seen Norma go all out like this."

"Ah, if she has not shared this information, perhaps she does not wish for you to know. I have much to do, so if you will please make yourself busy somewhere else, that would be best I think." Chef turned his back to me and resumed stirring his sauce.

"Aw, c'mon, please?" I sidled up to him. "Just a hint."

"Very well. I am told she has invited three restaurant reviewers, though only one has accepted. Also, an actor is coming all the way from Hollywood—Norma is enamored with the man and wishes to seduce him perhaps."

"Chef!" I couldn't believe he would talk about his employer in that way, but since I suspected Chef was secretly in love with Norma, perhaps he was jealous. "Is that all?"

"I believe the owner of Jean-Pierre's will also dine with us. He has tried to lure me away more than once. No doubt he is here to try again." He gave me a smug smile.

"You aren't thinking of leaving, are you?"

He sucked in a breath and whispered. "Ah, sadly, I find I cannot leave Mademoiselle Norma. I believe she has cast a spell on me."

Norma pushed open the door and hissed at

me. “There you are,” she scolded, as if she hadn’t sent me to the kitchen ten minutes earlier. “You need to make yourself presentable. Our guests will arrive in less than an hour.”

“Yes, Miss Thornley.” I hurried upstairs to freshen up and change.

When I came back downstairs, Norma instructed me how to properly greet the arrivals. “They’re not customers at my restaurant, they are guests in my home, and they should be treated as such. After you take their coats, offer them a martini or a glass of champagne. Omar will probably want Scotch, but that can’t be helped.”

“Omar?”

Her cheeks flushed with pleasure. “He’s a wonderful actor—divinely handsome, too. He will be a big star one day, mark my words.”

The doorbell soon rang, and when I opened it, a schoolfriend’s much older brother stood waiting. I blushed, remembering I’d once had a crush on him. He had dark hair, neatly parted on the side, rosy cheeks that gave him a boyish look, and horn-rimmed glasses.

“Joey?” I stared at him. “What are you doing here?” I’d heard that he had gone to work for the police force, but it hadn’t worked out.

He grabbed my arm and pulled me onto the

porch. "Shh. I've gone into business as a private detective. I'm undercover working a case, so don't tell anyone you know me. Tonight, I'm a successful businessman from Stockton." He smiled proudly and adjusted his tie, as if he'd done anything to earn that position.

"What do you mean you're working a case?"

"Someone has made an attempt on Miss Thornley's life, and she believes that someone will try again. She's invited the people she believes are the most likely to want her dead."

"Dead?" I stared at him in disbelief. "Who would want Norma Thornley dead?"

He puffed up his chest. "That's what I'm here to find out. It is possible they just want to put her out of business, but she's convinced her life is in danger, so here I am."

If someone really wanted Norma dead, I hoped she wasn't depending on this earnest but inexperienced young man to protect her.

THE REST OF THE GUESTS SOON ARRIVED STARTING with Omar, the actor, who arrived with a beautiful starlet on his arm he introduced as Dorothy. I nearly drooled over her incredibly soft sable coat as I took it from her while Norma poured Omar his scotch.

Clarence, the restaurant critic, was a short, round man with dark, thinning hair. Norma complimented him on his most recent review while pouring him a martini from a pitcher.

Norma's sister Barbara arrived next, looking chic in a simple black dress. She shoved her coat at me without a word, then headed straight for the drink cart where she poured herself a martini. After guzzling it down, she poured herself a second.

When the rival restaurant owner arrived, Norma hurried over and gave him a kiss on each cheek.

"Jean-Pierre, where is your wife?"

"Alas," he said in a French accent that sounded less than authentic to my ears, "she is not well and could not join us tonight. She sends her regrets and her best wishes to you, my dear."

A frown flashed on Norma's face before she plastered on a smile and offered him a drink. Glancing at the table set for eight, I had an idea why she wasn't happy that Jean-Pierre had come alone.

Norma cornered me by the coat closet. "You must dine with us."

"Me?" I asked. "I wouldn't know what to say to these people."

She glanced back at her guests then back at me, scrunching up her mouth before saying, "It can't be helped. You don't need to say much. I will seat you between Jean-Pierre and Clarence. All a pretty girl like you needs to do is smile, nod, and laugh at their jokes."

"I don't know…"

Her eyes narrowed. "You are being paid to work and you will do as I say. And I hope I don't need to tell you to be on your best behavior."

"Of course." My heart beat faster as excitement fought with nervousness. I couldn't believe that me, a lowly worker, would soon be sitting at a table with the sort of people who wouldn't normally give me the time of day.

I wanted to ask Norma about what Joey had told me, but she'd already taken me by the arm and led me to the others to introduce me.

"Irma is a family friend who helps me with the restaurant from time to time," she explained, no doubt not wanting to tell her guests she was paying me to fill the eighth seat.

Omar appeared by my side, reached for my hand, and kissed the back of it. "What a charming young lady. You must sit with me at dinner," he added with a wink.

Norma grabbed his arm. "Don't be silly. You're sitting with me, of course." She led him to his seat. As the hostess, she would sit at the head of the table and suggested Jean-Pierre sit on her right.

"Irma," she called out to me, sounding uncharacteristically friendly. "Come here, dear, and take your seat next to Jean-Pierre."

The restauranteur leered at me, and I wished I'd hadn't picked a low-cut dress to wear that day. Clarence, the restaurant critic, sat on the other side of me, as promised, and Barbara took her place at the foot of the table.

"Your drink is empty," Barbara said to Clarence, snatching his glass. "Here, take mine, I haven't even touched it. I've decided to switch to wine."

One of the waiters appeared out of nowhere. "White or red?"

"We're having roast turkey this evening, so white, of course."

"Of course, madam," he said and disappeared again.

When everyone had their drinks—even me, though I didn't plan to drink more than a sip of the wine I'd been served—Jean-Pierre proposed a toast.

"To Norma, who has managed to make a

name for herself and her restaurant here in the middle of nowhere. To your continued success."

"To your success," the others repeated and clinked their glasses together.

As the conversation resumed, Clarence made a choking sound and clutched his throat.

"Are you alright?" I hadn't seen him eat anything since we sat down so I didn't know what to do.

His cheeks reddened and he began to gasp for air. "Can't," he croaked. "Can't… breathe."

"It's the drink," Barbara cried out. "Someone tampered with the drink I gave him."

I glanced across the table at Joey who jumped out of his chair and came over to try to help the choking critic.

"I'll call for an ambulance." I hurried to the phone and called the operator.

As I asked the operator to connect me, I heard Barbara's frantic voice.

"That drink was meant for me. Someone tried to poison me."

As Clarence was loaded onto a gurney, I overheard Joey say to Norma, "I thought you were the one whose life was in danger."

Norma shook her head and said nothing while her dinner guest was carried out and loaded onto the ambulance.

"We need to call the police."

"No!" she hissed. "And you won't say anything about this incident, do you hear me? If word got out that our food and drink was tainted, no one would come to my restaurant. As it is, it will take a sizeable settlement to keep Clarence from ruining my reputation."

Food? This was the first I'd heard—then I remembered the herbs that had made their way into the kitchen.

Was someone trying to kill Barbara? Or Norma?

Omar and Dorothy made their excuses and left in the limousine that had been waiting in the driveway. Norma held her hand to her cheek where he'd kissed her as she watched him leave.

Barbara stood next to Norma. "He's a cad. He would have used you and tossed you aside."

"Ah, yes, you are most likely correct." Norma said. "But it would have been lovely as long as it lasted."

Barbara scowled in disapproval. "Someday, you need to settle down, Norma."

"Someday, perhaps, but not today."

"I'm going home to my husband where no

one is likely to try and poison me. Please don't invite me to dinner again. If you do, I shan't come."

As she walked away, Norma rolled her eyes, and I had to stop myself from laughing.

Jean-Pierre distracted Norma, and someone grabbed my elbow. Joey pulled me to the side of the room.

"I need your help," he whispered while keeping an eye on Norma and Jean-Pierre.

"I thought you said someone was out to get Norma. Why would someone want to poison Barbara?"

"I understand they co-own this Victorian home. It must be worth a pretty penny."

"Yes, but..." I began as my thoughts swum. "Who would kill both sisters for a house? There must be easier ways to get money. Besides, they have no blood relatives other than each other. If they both died, Barbara's husband would likely inherit both their estates."

"Tell me about her husband."

"He's a very successful banker. Do you really think he's sneaking into the kitchen to mess with the herbs? Besides, if Chef hadn't discovered the hemlock, anyone might have eaten it. If you were trying to kill Norma or Barbara—or both for that matter, that's a poor way to go about it."

He nodded thoughtfully. "You have a point. Maybe I've been looking at this the wrong way. If Norma or Barbara aren't the target, then who is?"

"No one." A theory began to form in my mind. "What if someone is trying to get Maison Rose closed down? If that is the case, then who would benefit?"

Joey peered past me at the most likely perpetrator. "Jean-Pierre."

"I agree. Who else?"

"Who else?" Joey asked. "What do you mean?"

"Haven't you ever read a detective story? There are always at least three suspects, and it almost never is the most likely person."

"Detective stories?" He scoffed. "This isn't a dime store novel. This is real life, and real criminals don't follow rules."

"Nevertheless, I think we should consider all the possibilities, especially since Jean-Pierre lives two hours away. It seems unlikely he's responsible for the earlier incidents."

Joey sighed. "I hadn't thought of that."

"What if Norma staged all this because she wanted to get rid of Clarence. So, she engineered these little incidents all leading up to tonight with you here to be a witness. Perhaps he planned to write a scathing review."

"You forget," he said smugly. "The poison was in Barbara's glass."

"Oh." I paused. I had forgotten. "Maybe Norma wanted to get rid of her sister. Have you seen them together? They're not exactly close."

"That would be a crafty plan. Claim someone is trying to kill you, and when someone else ends up dead, you'd likely be the last person suspected."

"If it weren't for the two of us."

He grinned. "Thanks for your help." His smile faded. "The problem is, Norma is the one who hired me. How do I go about proving she tried to kill her sister?"

"The more important question is—how do we keep her from trying again? Next time she might succeed."

"I'm going to have to go to the police," he said. "I don't care what Norma said."

"I'm sure that's for the best. Maybe you can ask them to can keep it quiet for now so she doesn't know you're onto her."

THE NEXT DAY, SHORTLY AFTER I ARRIVED FOR MY shift, a police officer arrived to question Norma. Clarence was on the mend and claimed that his hospitalization had nothing to do with anything he'd eaten or drunk while at Maison Rose. Norma must have provided a sizeable payoff to buy his silence.

"I don't understand why you are here bothering me." Norma sounded as innocent as a newborn baby, though I knew different.

"Strictly routine, ma'am."

Someone banged on the front door, and Norma called out to me. "Will you get that?"

I opened the door, and Barbara pushed past me. "I saw a police car. What's going on?" When she spotted the officer, she asked, "Did she tell you someone tried to kill me last night?"

Norma shot her sister daggers with her eyes. "This doesn't involve you."

The officer held up a hand to quiet Norma and asked Barbara, "What do you mean someone tried to kill you?"

"My drink was poisoned!" Barbara seemed pleased to have a chance to share her ordeal. "Thank goodness I didn't drink any of it. I gave it to Clarence since he'd finished his and I'd decided I didn't want it anymore."

A chill ran up my spine as a memory returned. I stepped forward. "But you'd asked for that drink twenty minutes earlier. You carried it around with you all that time without taking a single sip?"

"Hush," Barbara said. "No one asked you."

"I'm interested," the officer turned to me. "Please go on."

It all made sense now that I put the pieces together. "Norma, didn't Barbara want you to sell the house when she moved out?"

"So what?" Barbara said. "It didn't make sense for me to own half a house I wasn't ever going to live in again."

"And she resented you for having such a glamorous life while she's, well..." I didn't want to complete the sentence in front of Barbara.

Norma finished it for me. "While she's spending evenings with her boring, balding banker of a husband. She's taken every opportunity to put me down because of my lifestyle, but I've always known she was jealous."

"Jealous? Me?" Barbara's voice sounded high and shrill. "Of you? Running around like a tramp, embarrassing me with your antics and your men? Accepting gifts like a common—"

"Don't you dare say it." Norma stood with her nose mere inches from her sister. "I can't believe what a bitter woman you've become. You're the one who's been tainting the food, trying to make people sick, aren't you? I can't believe you hate me so much you would even poison poor Clarence. He could have died."

"There wasn't enough in the drink to kill him."

My mouth dropped open at her admission. The officer wasted no time slapping a pair of handcuffs on Barbara's hands.

"What do you think you're doing?" she shrieked.

"You're under arrest for poisoning Clarence Murphy. I'm taking you down to the station."

"You can't do that." She squirmed, trying to get away from the officer, but he held on tightly.

"Watch me." He grabbed her by the elbow and led her to the door.

Norma followed them outside, saying, "Don't worry, Barbara. I'll call our lawyer and get you released in no time. Chin up."

After she watched the police car drive away with her sister, Norma came back inside.

"I hope you've learned your lesson to stay out of what doesn't concern you, Irma," she said in a scolding tone.

"But..." I barely knew what to say. "She tried to ruin your reputation and get your restaurant closed down. How can you say I should have stayed out of it? She might have killed one of your customers. She might have killed you."

"Pish posh. That never would have happened." She walked to the phone and picked it up, but before she dialed it held the receiver in her hand with a faraway look in her eye. "Family is everything. If I can't trust my own sister, who can I trust?"

PRESENT TIME

APRIL

I stared at Irma. "Norma really said that? After everything that happened?"

"Yep. Of course, she knew absolutely nothing about trust. And the last person she should have trusted was Barbara, especially after what happened. If the rumors are true, then Barbara is the one who pushed her down the stairs."

A crashing sound came from the front room.

"What was that?" I hurried to see what had caused the sound, hoping that nothing valuable or irreplaceable had been broken.

Jennifer and Irma followed me into the dining room where a heap of crystals and broken glass lay in the middle of the floor.

"My beautiful chandelier!" I'd splurged on

two matching chandeliers for my tearoom, and I'd never regretted it. They gave the room a special ambience and I loved them. I collapsed into a chair and covered my face with my hands, not wanting to see how bad the damage was.

"It's not too terribly awful," Jennifer said tentatively.

"Not terribly awful at all." Irma sounded positively cheerful. "It looks much worse than it is, April. Come and see."

She was right. My breathing returned to normal when a closer inspection showed that the damage was limited to several broken bulbs.

"I'm sorry about that," Irma said. "I guess we need a new rule in this house."

I nodded, and Jennifer, Irma, and I said at once:

"We don't talk about Norma."

READ ON FOR JENNIFER'S FAVORITE THANKSGIVING recipe and another Haunted Tearoom story!

GELATIN PRETZEL SALAD

INGREDIENTS:

- 1 6 oz. package orange-flavored gelatin (can also use cranberry)
- 1 cup boiling water
- 1 can (11 oz) mandarin orange segments, drained, juice reserved
- Juice from mandarin orange segments plus enough water to equal 1 cup
- 2 ½ cups salted pretzel sticks (measured before crushing)
- ½ cup (8 Tablespoons) unsalted butter, melted
- 4 Tablespoons granulated sugar (use 2 Tablespoons at a time)

- 1 package (8 oz) cream cheese, softened
- 1 container (8 oz) Cool Whip or other frozen whipped topping, thawed

DIRECTIONS:

1. Pre-heat oven to 350 F (175 C)
2. Combine flavored gelatin (Jell-O or other brand) with 1 cup boiling water and stir until dissolved. Add mandarin orange juice/water and refrigerate until partially set—about 1 ½ to 1 ¾ hours.
3. Grease 13" x 9" glass baking dish or spray with cooking spray.
4. Put the pretzels in a plastic bag and smash into small pieces and crumbs.
5. Melt butter, mix in 2 Tablespoons sugar, then add crushed pretzels. Spread the mixture into the baking dish, pressing it into an even layer. Bake at 350 F (175 C) for 10 minutes. Put in refrigerator to cool.
6. Beat cream cheese and the remaining 2 Tablespoons sugar on med/high speed until fluffy and white. Fold in Cool

Whip (or other whipped topping) until blended.

7. Spread cream cheese mixture over cooled pretzels, spreading to the edges to seal. Refrigerate 30 minutes.
8. Finely chop mandarin orange segments and stir into partially set gelatin. Carefully pour gelatin mixture over cream cheese layer. Refrigerate 8 hours or overnight.
9. Cut into squares and serve as a side dish or light dessert.

TEA IS FOR TINSEL

A HAUNTED TEAROOM CHRISTMAS STORY

CHRISTMAS IN SERENITY COVE

With a name like April May, everyone expected me to be cheerful and bright like a ray of sunshine, and I generally lived up to that expectation. But here I was, serving tea, scones, and dainty sandwiches to the guests in my tearoom, and the smile on my face felt pasted on.

I'd always loved Christmas, even when Santa left nothing under the tree. No matter—there were cookies to bake, carols to sing, and at least a zillion Christmas movies to watch snuggled up to my mom on the sofa with a cup of hot cocoa—extra marshmallows of course.

My first Christmas in the seaside town of Serenity Cove would also be my first big holiday since my mother had passed away. Running

SereniTea tearoom kept me busy, but I still missed Mom terribly.

My mother had little money for decorations or presents when I was a child, and I spent many a Christmas morning disappointed. She'd see me pouting and grab my hand, pulling me to my feet. "April May, what do you have to be sad about? You have a voice for singing and two legs for dancing." She'd begin singing "Jingle Bells" off-key at the top of her lungs, and we'd dance around the living room until I collapsed in a fit of giggles.

With two weeks until Christmas Day, I found myself reflecting on my mother. I shut out the less pleasant memories, doing my best to focus on the positive.

My lovely Victorian house had become the home I'd never had growing up, filled with warmth and the scents of fresh baked scones and pastries. The first floor served as the tearoom, with the huge front room filled with round tables covered in floral tablecloths, displays of teapots and teacups on antique hutches, and the ornate crystal chandeliers I'd splurged on in an impulsive moment.

The front windows displayed a view of the ocean, beautiful and majestic. On warm days, I'd open a window to let the salty sea breeze float through the room. I found it more relaxing than any music I might pipe in. I still marveled at being able to sit on my front porch and watch the sun set while seagulls bobbed and dove overhead hoping to find scraps of food left behind by tourists.

The biggest gift I'd received when I moved to Serenity Cove came in the form of friends who felt more like family than my own relatives ever had.

My young assistant, Jennifer Skillings, interrupted my trip down memory lane as she carried the last of the dishes into the kitchen. She'd lost her mother at a young age, and although I'd never be able to take her place, I'd become something of a surrogate mother to her. I'd never had a child of my own, but if I had, I would have been lucky to have one as precocious, curious, and kind as Jennifer.

"The last guest has left, and the front door is locked tight." She took off her apron, revealing a festive red dress, green tights, and pointed elf shoes.

"I'm surprised we were so busy today." When I moved to a town with a population of 963 earlier in the year, I knew we would have to depend on summer tourism for most of our business, and I'd been glad to find that we got visitors other times of the year as well. "Do we always get so many tourists over the holidays?"

She grinned with pride. "We got an award last year for the best decorated town in the entire county, and we got a lot more visitors after that."

I'd driven through town after dark and it seemed as if nearly every house in town had colorful lights and blow-up Santas with fake snow everywhere.

Jennifer continued talking as we finished cleaning the kitchen. "City Hall goes all out with a fifty-foot tree."

"Fifty feet! Is it real?"

"It is, and I'm not sure how I feel about it, but in my heart of hearts, I really love it." Jennifer put the last of the dishes into the dishwasher. "Oh! Maybe we can get our own Christmas tree on the way back from the tree lighting ceremony. If it's not too late, I bet the lot will still be open."

"I don't think I'm going to the tree lighting." As I hand washed the last of the teacups, I considered making an excuse. Instead, I gave the real reason, at least part of it. "I'm just not in the mood."

"Oh April," she said with a sigh. "That's why you should come. If lighting a huge Christmas tree and singing carols doesn't get you in the spirit, then I don't know what will. There's even an ice-skating rink, and there'll be plenty of hot cider and cocoa. It'll be fun!"

Her hopeful and pleading face nearly made me change my mind. "Maybe next time."

"Next time?" Jennifer's rosy-red mouth turned into a pout. "You mean next year?"

"Yes." I gave her a playful smile. "I'll put it on my calendar."

I'd just put a batch of gingerbread people into the oven, and the aroma filled the warm kitchen. "Will you have time to help decorate the gingerbread before you leave?" I asked. "They have to cool before we ice them."

Her face lit up. "I always have time for cookie decorating. Speaking of decorating, I found a box of Christmas stuff in the attic, so while we're waiting for the cookies, I thought I'd decorate the tearoom. Wanna help?"

I sucked in a breath and let it out. "I'm going to finish cleaning up in here." I hated disappointing her, but decorating brought back memories of my mother digging out a box of dusty trimmings and ornaments that we'd arrange around our tiny apartment.

Once Jennifer had left the room, I clapped my hands together and told myself, "Snap out of it, April."

Chef Emile Toussaint shimmered into view.

My ghostly companion, a French chef who'd died sixty years earlier, seemed destined to spend eternity in my kitchen giving me cooking tips. I'd discovered him haunting my house soon after I'd moved in, and after the initial shock, I'd gotten used to his presence, eventually finding I enjoyed his company.

"Why are you snapping?" he asked in an annoyed tone of voice as if I'd interrupted him from something important.

"I'm just not in the Christmas spirit this year." The timer went off and I transferred the cookies to a rack to cool. Once done with that task, I poured myself a cup of tea and took a seat at the kitchen island for a well-deserved break.

"Ah, the ginger cookies, *non*? I do not smell the ginger."

"I went light on the ginger," I said before realizing he probably couldn't smell them at all. I wondered if that bothered him after a lifetime of tasting and smelling his own wonderful food cooking. "Did you see I made your recipe for pecan cocoons?" My mother had always called them snowball cookies, since that's what the round, buttery cookies looked like after being coated in two layers of powdered sugar, but his recipe was nearly identical. I'd also heard them called Mexican or Italian wedding cookies.

He glanced at the plate of snowy-looking cookies. "My mother baked them every Christmas. I would help roll them in the powdery sugar and my fingertips would become coated and sticky. Of course, I would lick them clean." He smiled wistfully at the happy memory.

"What was Christmas like when you were growing up in Louisiana?" I knew his family hadn't had much, but for a child, the season wasn't about money.

"Bonfires were lit along the rivers on the levees," he began, and his original Cajun accent began to slip through his carefully cultivated French accent. "They lit the way for Papa Noel and his skiff as he flew across the sky on his way—"

"His skiff?" I interrupted. "Isn't that a boat?"

"Mais oui," he said with a smile. "Your Santa Claus may travel in a sled, but Papa Noel, he travels in a flying skiff."

After a moment of thought, I said, "I suppose that makes about as much sense as a sled with flying reindeer."

Jennifer returned to the kitchen with two boxes. "This came in the mail," she said, handing me the smaller package.

I examined the label. "It's from Lulu." My mood brightened, wondering what my new sister-in-law had sent me. I cut the packing tape and opened the box. Under yards of tissue paper, I uncovered an old tree topper, which I recognized immediately.

"There's a note." Jennifer picked up a folded, yellowed paper that had fallen onto the floor and handing it to me.

As I unfolded it, the childish scrawl made me smile. "It's a letter to Santa." I read the letter, first to myself and then out loud. "Dear Santa. Please bring me a Strawberry Shortcake doll. And please bring Mommy some money so she will be happy and we can have a good Christmas. Sincerely, April May."

"How sweet," Jennifer said, a wistful smile on her face.

Setting the note aside, I picked up the homemade angel and turned it over in my hands. My mother had made it from a cheap doll's head. I'd always found her a little creepy with her plastic hair, huge blue eyes, and tiny red pout. Its midsection was a ping pong ball covered in glued-on glitter and lit from within by a little bulb. A small, upside-down chandelier shade served as the angel's skirt.

No wonder my brother didn't want it. I must have been six years old when she first placed it on our tree, and I took an immediate dislike to it.

My brother, thirteen years older than me, had already moved out on his own, and probably didn't even remember it.

"That's totally adorable," Jennifer said with surprising enthusiasm. "Is it handmade?"

How there could be any doubt I couldn't imagine. "Can you tell?" I said sarcastically.

"Yes, but it's so, so… retro. And we have our first decoration for our tree. That is if you're okay with me picking it out without you."

"I'm not sure." I meant that I wasn't sure I wanted a tree, but Jennifer must have thought otherwise.

"That's okay," she said. "We'll go together one day next week. That way we can go when the sun's out so we can see better. I can't wait to get it and start decorating."

I changed the subject. "What's in the other box?"

"Decorations. They must be super old. I blew off the dust before I dragged it downstairs and nearly choked." She opened the box and pulled out items wrapped in yellowed tissue paper. She unwrapped one vintage ornament after another setting them on the counter, getting more excited with each reveal. "These are going to look wonderful on our tree."

She handed me one and I turned it over in my

hand, admiring the vibrant colors. "These look really old."

"Did you know the tradition of using glass ornaments began in Germany in the eighteen hundreds? Before that, trees were decorated with nuts and berries and things like that. These are probably from the 1940's." Among her other attributes, Jennifer was something of an antiques expert, after working with her father in his antique shop. "Check it out." She grabbed a handful of tinsel and held it up to show me. The metallic sheen glittered in the light. "It's heavy! It must be real, old-fashioned tinsel—not the cheap plastic kind we have now."

"Put that down!"

Jennifer dropped the tinsel like it was radioactive.

"Sorry! I may have overreacted." I gave her an apologetic smile. "Tinsel used to be made out of silver, which, as you might imagine was quite expensive. It also tarnished. So, they started using lead foil. It was a great solution, except, you know, for the lead."

"Oh." Jennifer hurried over to the sink to wash her hands.

"I'm pretty sure it's only toxic with prolonged exposure, but it's probably best we don't put it on the tree."

"What a shame." She pulled a pair of tongs from a drawer and lifted a few strands of tinsel for a closer look. "It's so pretty and shiny."

A rap on the back door interrupted us, and Irma Vargas, the owner of the Mermaid Café, appeared in the doorway to the storeroom. She wore an oversized, green-striped sweater with a big red stocking on the front.

She frowned at my casual outfit. "I hope you're changing into something more festive."

"Is there an ugly sweater contest tonight?" I asked. "Because you're a contender."

She stuck her tongue out at me. "This sweater is both festive and practical." She reached into the stocking and pulled out a bottle of whiskey. "In case it gets cold."

"I'm going to skip the tree lighting," I said. "I have a lot to do. But you can help us decorate the gingerbread people if you want."

Irma's attention had been drawn to the tree topper lying on the island. "What the heck is that?"

Jennifer jumped in, possibly thinking I'd be insulted if Irma insulted my mother's creation. "April's mother made it. Isn't it adorable?"

"Adorable isn't the word I'd use," Irma said.

No one spoke for several moments, and then I said, "Hideous?"

"No, it's not—" Jennifer began.

"Grotesque?" Irma suggested.

"No, it's—" Jennifer tried again.

I interrupted her with, "Repellant."

"Bride of Chucky?" Irma said, and I burst into laughter.

"Stop it, you two!" Jennifer cried out. "This decoration was hand made by April's mother. I will not stand here and listen to both of you saying such horrible things about it."

"Well, sit down then," Irma said, and Jennifer gave her a glare.

"You're right," I said. "My mother was very proud of her. We didn't have much money for decorations back then. It really was pretty creative of her to make this—I think she copied something she saw in a magazine, believe it or not."

Irma met my gaze and we both did our best not to break into laughter again.

"Let's decorate some cookies." I put the angel back in her box and set her aside. I'd decide what to do with her later.

I'd filled three piping bags with red, green, and white icing, which I set on the island, along with sprinkles, colored sugar, and edible white pearls. Setting a paper plate with a cookie in front of Jennifer and another in front of Irma, I sat down and got to work on my own.

Jennifer had found a photo on her phone that she did her best to painstakingly recreate. I became distracted watching Irma, whose gingerbread man appeared to be sporting a speedo. She added a bow tie to his neck.

"It's a Chippendale's gingerbread dancer," she explained.

I bit my lower lip to keep from laughing and studied Jennifer's creation.

"Your gingerbread man is really cute," I said.

"It's a gingerbread person," she said. "They're gender neutral."

Irma leaned over the island to get a closer look, then pointed at the cookie person's crotch. "Oh, yeah? Then what's that?"

Jennifer scowled back at Irma. "That's a button!"

No longer able to hold back my laughter, I turned away to keep from spitting on any of the cookies.

Chef stood in the corner shaking his head as if he disapproved, but his smile told me he was enjoying watching and listening to our silliness.

By the time I'd decorated a dozen cookies, Irma and Jennifer had finished two each. For them, it was about having fun, so I didn't complain.

Jennifer glanced at the clock. "We need to go soon. Do you want me to help you pack up the cookies?"

"These will need to dry for several hours," I explained. "I have a batch I made yesterday that's packed up for you to take." I handed her a box I'd filled with various Christmas cookies I'd made the day before. Jennifer looked disappointed, so I added, "Do you want to take yours with you? I can put them in a plastic container so they don't get ruined."

"No, that's okay." She brightened. "I'll save them to give to my grandma."

"Good idea," Irma said. "Just be sure to explain about the button. You wouldn't want her to get the wrong idea."

MRS. HIGGLESWORTH AND MISS PAISLEY

The days flew by as Serenity Cove had an unexpected influx of visitors. With little to do in our small town, most of them found their way into our teashop. I'd expanded the gift display, and we nearly sold out of many of our most popular teapots, teacups, and other ceramic items. Our "tea shirts" also proved to be popular, much to Jennifer's delight, since she'd suggested carrying them.

Two days before Christmas, we still hadn't gotten around to getting a tree. I didn't see why it was so important since we were going to be closed for the next five days and Jennifer planned to spend time with her family.

While I cooked and baked in preparation for the day's customers, I sent Jennifer to pick up a few items at the grocery store. She returned with a six-foot tall, bedraggled looking tree. As I helped her carry it in, all I could think of was all the pine needles I'd be sweeping up for weeks.

I tried to convince Jennifer to let me put it in the study. "We don't have time to decorate it, and it looks a little pathetic with no ornaments."

Jennifer's face fell. "You don't like it."

"No, that's not it." I thought I'd made it clear I didn't really want a tree, but I didn't want to hurt Jennifer's feelings or dampen her Christmas spirit. "Once it's decorated, I'm sure it will look great. I'll see what's in the attic and decorate it tonight or tomorrow. I don't have much else to do, anyway."

"How about we put it right here?" Jennifer maneuvered the tree to a corner near the kitchen door. "This way you can see it when you sit in front of the fire, but it's not too close. We don't want it getting dried out."

I couldn't imagine the tree getting any drier than it already was. "Or catching on fire," I mumbled.

"What?" Jennifer asked.

"I said, that's a great spot for it."

Jennifer hurried into the kitchen and returned with the angel, carefully placing it on top of the tree. She took a step back and said, "Perfect."

I bit my tongue.

We had only one reservation for afternoon tea, and as the day rolled on, only a few others dropped in.

Jennifer glanced at the reservation list. "Mayor Gasden is coming for tea?"

"Party of four," I confirmed. "They're running late, so I have my fingers crossed they won't show. I wouldn't mind closing early."

Mayor Wanda Gasden had been a thorn in my side since we first laid eyes on her. She had similar feelings for me, especially since I'd prevented her from turning the library into a food court.

The mayor arrived nearly a half hour late. Tall and blonde, the middle-aged woman strode through the door with her entourage in tow. Her assistant Pauline hovered nearby, her curly auburn bob only partially controlled by a black headband. I didn't recognize the two other women.

"Welcome back, Mayor Gasden," I said in greeting. "Nice to see you again, Pauline."

The mayor responded with a curt nod and introduced her other guests. "Allow me to introduce Mrs. James Higglesworth, my co-chair on the arts committee." Mrs. Higglesworth looked to be in her sixties, with tightly curled, dark gray hair. She wore a gray skirt suit, giving her a monotone look, reminding me of granite.

"Nice to meet you," I said, surprised to learn our little town had an arts committee.

"And this is her assistant, Miss Paisley."

"Call me Jane," the woman said with a friendly smile. She appeared to be thirty going on fifty. Black-framed glasses partially hid her unlined face, and she wore a floral skirt and pink embroidered sweater. I glanced at her running shoes, and Mrs. Higglesworth noticed.

"I've told her a thousand times that gym shoes are not appropriate attire for daily wear," she said. "But does she listen to me?"

Jane shrugged, obviously tired of hearing the older woman's criticism.

I showed the women to a table, but before they were seated, Mrs. Higglesworth pointed at the tree in the back of the room. "Is that a Michael André?"

"Huh?" I had no idea what she might be talking about. "Are you talking about the tree?"

She gave me a patronizing look. "The *finial d'bare*." When she didn't get a response, she clarified further. "The tree topper."

"Oh, yes. My mother," I stopped before saying

my mother made it, not willing to have it mocked by this woman. "My mother left it to me."

"Your mother had excellent taste," she said. "Michael André was a brilliant artist in the nineteen-fifties, second only to Andy Warhol in his inventiveness and creativity. He found beauty in items that others disposed of."

"Fascinating." It was the only thing I could think of to say. Did she really think my mother's craft project was a work of art? Once she realized it was homemade, I knew she'd dismiss it without a second thought.

WHISK

We finally said goodbye to Mayor Gasden and her group, and I flipped the sign to closed. As Jennifer and I carried dishes and trays to the kitchen, I stopped next to the tree.

"Can you believe Mrs. Higglesworth thinks that my mother's tree topper is an artwork?" I asked.

"I already knew it," Jennifer said. "I don't need some snob to tell me what art is."

I took one more look at the ornament, doing my best to see it through an art collector's eyes. I shrugged and returned to my cleanup tasks.

"You're coming to the community center for the party, aren't you?" Jennifer asked hopefully.

"Santa will be there, not to mention all the hot chocolate and cookies you can eat and drink."

I shook my head. "I'm beat. You don't mind taking my contribution with you, do you?" I'd baked several dozen cookies for the event, and they were boxed and ready to go.

Jennifer's disappointed expression almost made me change my mind. "I suppose not," she said. "But next year—"

"Next year, I'll attend every event from Thanksgiving to New Year's. I promise." I opened the dishwasher and began filling it with dirty plates. "What are you planning to do with your free time for the next several days?"

"My grandmother wants me to stay over, and we're going to have a holiday movie marathon," she said. "We're starting tonight with *Miracle on 34th Street*. Tomorrow will be *It's a Wonderful Life* and *Die Hard*. I can't believe that tomorrow is Christmas Eve already."

"*Die Hard* is a Christmas movie?" I asked. Maybe there was another movie by that name I hadn't seen.

She laughed. "That's what my grandmother said. My mother and I used to watch it every year."

"It's nice you have your grandmother back in your life."

Jennifer must have heard the wistfulness in my voice, because she asked if I'd like to join them. "We've got plenty of food and room on the sofa."

"Thanks," I said. "I'm looking forward to some alone time. And Irma's coming over for breakfast on Christmas. Why don't you and Helen come? They'll be plenty of food here too."

"I'll ask her, but she may have other plans." She paused, then added, "But I'll come for sure. Would you mind if I went upstairs to pack up a few things?"

"Go ahead. There's not much left to do. I just have to decide what to do with the leftovers." I'd put some in the freezer and munch on the rest that evening.

She soon clomped back down the stairs with her suitcase, and after giving me a hug, left me alone in the house.

Chef Emile spoke, reminding me of his presence. "You are alone again?"

His comment stung, but I put on a brave smile. "Not with you here, I'm not. And Whisk, of course."

Whisk, the Bengal cat who lived in the attic, rarely came downstairs. Before I bought the house, he'd survived on his hunting skills. I took a scoop of food and a bottle of water and climbed the two flights of stairs to the attic.

Even more independent than the typical cat, Whisk often hid when I brought him his food, but I could usually coax him out. I enjoyed visiting with him when he emerged to greet me, and I'd learned he was a good listener.

I filled his bowls and called out to him. He appeared quickly from behind a pile of boxes. Perhaps the day's hunting hadn't been fruitful, or perhaps I was finally turning him into a house cat.

He strolled leisurely toward his food, and then froze, his whiskers twitching and his tail sharply swinging back and forth.

"Did you hear something?" These old houses were full of noises, especially in the evening as they settled. As I stopped to listen, a tree scraped against the side of the house. "I'll see about getting the trees trimmed. I don't like that sound either."

"Mrraw," he said.

"What would you like Santa to bring you, Whisk?" I asked.

He strode over to his bed and nuzzled it.

"A new bed? I can arrange that." I'd make sure the pet store in Somerton was open tomorrow before driving all the way out there. Maybe I'd get him a catnip mouse, too.

Whisk climbed onto my lap just as something crashed below. He dug his claws into my legs as he leaped off me. I turned in time to see him scurry out the attic window.

Grabbing a heavy candlestick, I hurried to the second floor with my heart pounding in my ears. As I reached the landing, a figure in black dashed past the tearoom tables and out the front door, leaving it wide open. I rushed to the door to see if they had a car, thinking I could get the plate number, but there was no sign of them or their car.

The wind caught the screen door, banging it against the side of the house. As I stepped onto the porch to close it, a cold gust of air rushed past me. As soon as I'd locked up the front door, I dashed to the kitchen to call the police station.

A strange voice answered. "Deputy Timothy Bonner speaking."

"I've had a break-in," I blurted out.

"Who is this?"

"This is April May at the Serenity Tearoom. 525 Ocean View Drive."

"April May?" he repeated.

"Yes, it's my real name." I wasn't in the mood

for the questions I always got when I told people my name.

"Deputy Molina told me about you," he said. "You might even say he warned me."

I sighed and walked back into the tearoom while I spoke to him. "Someone just ran out of my house. I don't know if they stole anything, but..." My voice trailed off as I looked at the bare Christmas tree.

The angel was gone.

TINY

While waiting for Deputy Bonner, I called Irma, asking her to come over and keep me company. Not that I was afraid of being alone, of course. Well, maybe a little.

As soon as she arrived, I said, "I'm going to check the safe." The wall safe in the study held a fortune in jewelry that the previous owners had hidden in the house.

"Don't you think you should wait until the police arrive?" Irma asked. "Hey, Molina's on vacation. Who's on their way?"

"Deputy Bonner."

"So, Tiny's back in town," she said with a sly grin while I poured her a cup of tea.

"Tiny?"

"Yeah, that's what everyone calls him. Have since he was a kid. He grew up here, you know."

The doorbell rang, and I went to meet the deputy. I got the joke right away. Just like a bald man's friends might call him Curly, Tiny was six and a half feet tall and at least three hundred pounds.

I introduced myself and got right to the point. "They must have been breaking into the safe looking for the jewels."

"Did they succeed?" he asked.

"Irma didn't want me to go in the study." I left out the part where I didn't want to go in there myself. "That's where the wall safe is."

I led him to the study door and stepped aside while he drew his gun and opened the door. He called out to give us the all clear.

When I entered the room, I held my breath, but let it out when I saw the landscape painting still on the wall covering the wall safe. Nothing in the room seemed out of place. Just to be sure, I lifted the painting from the wall, and opened the safe, checking the contents. Everything was right where it belonged.

The deputy led us back to the tearoom. "What else of value might a burglar have been after?"

"I can't think of a thing," I said. "I mean, we have some really nice teapots, but I can't imagine that was what they were after." I stared at the bare tree and felt a lump in the pit of my stomach.

The deputy asked me to show him around so he could determine how the burglar entered, even though I admitted I might have left the front door unlocked when I went to the attic.

"Too many residents never lock their doors until they go to sleep at night," the deputy groused. "The intruder must have assumed you were at the holiday bazaar at the community center with everyone else. Why weren't you?"

Not sure why he asked, I simply said, "I was tired."

"You keep looking at the tree," Deputy Bonner said. "Did the intruders steal all the decorations?"

I stopped and stared at him, wondering if he was teasing. "Well, actually…"

"Yes?" he prompted.

"My assistant just brought the tree home earlier today, and there was only one thing on it —a tree topper. Now it's missing."

"A tree topper?" he repeated. "Was it valuable?"

I managed a weak smile. "It was homemade. I think my mother saw a picture of one in a magazine and tried to copy it. I confess I thought it was ugly, but now that it's missing, I feel like I've lost something of her."

"Maybe someone thought it was valuable," he said. "Do you think that's possible?"

I shrugged. "Mrs. Higglesworth thought a famous artist had made it, but I can't imagine anyone thinking it was worth anything after they got a close look."

The deputy didn't seem to be in a hurry to rush back to the station, so I offered him a cup of tea and some cookies, which he accepted. He dutifully took my description of the tree topper. After he left with a bag of extra cookies, I locked up and armed the alarm system.

CHEF EMILE

My house felt empty and far too quiet except for the strange noises the old Victorian made. The wind blew tree branches against the side of the house, making an eerie scratching sound.

A little shiver ran through me, but I knew how to warm up. I soon made myself a cup of hot cocoa with cinnamon, extra marshmallows, and a shot of Irish Cream. I set it on a tray with about a dozen homemade cookies and climbed to the second-floor parlor, which I used as an office and den.

Setting down the tray, I perused the bookcase for something to read. Jennifer had filled it with classic books she'd found in the attic. My eyes lingered on *Wuthering Heights*, *Jane Eyre*, and *The*

Great Gatsby, but none of them appealed to me. I pulled out a thin volume and read the title: *A Christmas Carol* by Charles Dickens.

Once I got comfortable on the sofa with the book, I changed my mind. I wasn't in the mood for a ghost story, especially one extolling the virtues of Christmas spirit. Instead, I turned on the TV, hoping to find a movie to distract me from my solitude. *A Christmas Carol* with Jim Carrey came on, and I chuckled. I wondered what Dickens would say about all the versions of his tale.

I flicked the remote to the next channel where I came upon *Mr. Magoo's Christmas Carol*. I flicked past three different movie versions of the Charles Dickens classic until I came upon *Scrooged* with Bill Murray.

Carol Kane's performance in the movie was guaranteed to bring a laugh, so I leaned back and wrapped my hands around the mug of hot cocoa, enjoying the warmth.

The wind kicked up and blew the windows open, so I got up to close them, grumbling about the old house and its maintenance needs. With them locked up tight, I turned to go back to my comfy spot, only to be startled by a familiar apparition.

Chef Emile Toussaint stood in the doorway,

dressed as always in his white jacket and chef's hat. I'd never known him to leave the kitchen before. I didn't think he had the ability.

"Have you always been able to leave the kitchen?" I asked. "Are there any other secrets you're keeping from me?"

"*Ma chère,* we can speak of secrets another time. Tonight, we speak of memories, of joy and sadness, and of what is to become of you."

"Huh?" Chef wasn't typically so cryptic.

"You shall be visited by three spirits," he began.

"Oh!" I said cheerfully. "I know this one. Christmas Past, Christmas Present, and Christmas Future."

"*Mais oui,* but you steal my lightning."

"I think you mean thunder."

He sighed in frustration. "I had more to say, but it seems as if you know the story."

"Yeah," I said. "There are like fifty versions of it playing on TV right now. Want to have a seat and watch with me? I decided to watch *Scrooged* since it's the funniest of them. A Christmas Carol is kind of a downer, really, until you get to the end and the whole 'God bless us, everyone' part."

"Listen carefully. You have lost something."

"Yes, I know. My mother's tree topper." I'd never seen his eyes so full of pity, and I didn't like it. "Though it's not really lost. Someone stole it. Why would someone do such a thing?"

"You have lost... *ton esprit de Noël*. It has left a hole in your heart that must be filled, or it will eat your soul from the inside out."

"Wow." I stared at his somber face. "That's pretty dramatic, don't you think? There will be plenty of other Christmases. Just let me sit this one out, okay?"

"*Non*. There is never as much time as you think. This I know well." He shimmered and disappeared.

"Sheesh. I wonder what that was all about." I went back to my movie, but I must have fallen asleep. Someone was shaking my shoulder.

"Wake up," the voice said. A male voice.

My eyes flew open, and I jumped at the sight of a man with wild hair and a goatee wearing an old-fashioned three-piece suit and bow tie. "Who are you?"

He straightened up and threw his shoulders back haughtily. "You do not recognize me?" he asked in an English accent.

"Should I?" I felt the book next to me and picked it up. On the back was a portrait of the man standing in front of me.

It was Charles Dickens.

THE GHOST OF CHRISTMAS PAST

"You're Charles Dickens? *The* Charles Dickens, the one who wrote *A Christmas Carol*?"

"Is there another?"

If I did a quick online search, I'd probably find thousands of other Charles Dickens in the world, but I kept that information to myself. "No, just you. So, what brings you here to Serenity Cove, California?"

"Tonight, I will be your guide to the past." He took a deep bow.

"You're my Ghost of Christmas Past?" When he nodded, I added, "I'm honored."

"As you should be. Shall we proceed?"

"Proceed? Where?"

"Why, to the past, of course. Arise, please." He

held out his arm as if he were about to escort me to a ball.

Not wanting to be rude, I stood and laid my hand on his elbow. A whooshing sound filled my ears as the room spun, slowly at first, then faster and faster. I held on tightly as the years flashed before my eyes in reverse. For a moment, I panicked—wasn't that what people said happened when you died?

We landed with a thunk in a tiny apartment. I recognized the dingy gold brocade sofa right away. My mother had found it by the side of the road one day and talked a stranger into helping her carry it home. Christmas songs played on the radio and the aroma of vanilla and cinnamon told me cookies were baking.

The front door opened. A woman slipped inside and tiptoed to a small tree. I recognized my mother's tree topper. The woman's silvery voice called out, "I'm home," and when she turned, I saw her face. The sight of my mother took my breath away. She looked so young, but the real surprise was the girl who emerged from the kitchen with a tray of cookies.

It was nine-year-old me.

"Happy Christmas, my little ape," my mother said.

I used to hate it when she called me that, but to my adult ears it sounded wonderful.

"It's not Christmas yet," young April said, then her mouth dropped open. "What did you do to your hair?"

My mother's mouth tightened, but only for a moment. She forced a smile and said, "I cut it. It will grow back."

I turned to my ghost guide. "I forgot about the year she cut her hair." My mother had always been so proud of her long, wavy hair that fell past her waist.

"Watch and listen," he ordered.

The younger me said, "But you said you'd never cut your hair. Never ever."

"And that's why you should never say never. Remember that!" She took the tray of cookies from the child and set them on the table. "Want to open your presents?"

"Presents? I have presents?" She looked from my mother to the tree and back again. "Presents is plural, and that means more than one." She hesitated. "Doesn't it?"

"Yes, sweetheart," my mother said. I could see her fighting back tears, but my younger self couldn't take her eyes off the gifts under the tree.

"But I didn't get you a present," the child said.

"Yes, you did. You made me cookies."

The younger me grinned with excitement and pride. No wonder I loved baking. Once upon a time, I'd had little else to offer.

My mother grabbed the child's hands. Singing along to "Jingle Bells" as it played on the radio, the two danced around the room, and finally fell on the sofa laughing.

As I watched them, I felt a tear roll down my cheek. "She sold her hair, didn't she? She sold it so she could buy me presents." I wiped the tear away. "I never realized it until right now."

Charles Dickens' smile told me I was right. He held out his arm again for me to take.

"No, let me stay here longer," I pleaded. "We're going to open presents and eat cookies and play games. I'm not ready to go."

He held out his arm again.

"I love you, Mom." I blew her a kiss, and reluctantly took the spirit's arm.

THE GHOST OF CHRISTMAS PRESENTS

Moments or hours later—I wasn't sure—I woke up on the sofa. On the TV, Carol Kane slugged Bill Murray, then said, "Sometimes, the truth is painful."

Boy, wasn't that right. As I worked the crick out of my neck, I mumbled, "That was some weird dream."

From outside the door, a low voice called, "Ho, ho, ho."

Had Jennifer lured Santa Claus here in an attempt to get me out of my holiday funk? I certainly hoped not, but I had no other explanation.

The parlor door flew open, and Santa appeared in all his glory "Ho, ho, ho! Merry Christmas!"

I looked him up and down, admiring his velveteen jacket and polished boots. His beard even looked real, and his cheeks could hardly be rosier.

"Hi, Santa."

"Ho, ho, ho!"

"Look, I appreciate the visit," I told him, "but I'd just like to have a quiet evening and finish watching my movie if it's all right with you."

"Cookies!" Santa's eyes lit up and he dove for the plate, stuffing all the remaining cookies in his mouth at once.

"Hey! Those were my cookies." As I watched him with his cheeks full and crumbs on his beard, I began to worry. "How'd you get in? I locked the front door and set the alarm."

Santa smiled, his eyes twinkling. "Ghosts don't need to be let in."

"Ghosts?" My heart sank. "But if you're a ghost then that means... Santa Claus is dead?"

He laughed heartily. "Santa Claus will never be dead as long as there are those who believe in Christmas spirit. I have taken the form of jolly St. Nick, but I think you know who I really am."

I stared at him. "Nope. I really don't."

"I'm the ghost of Christmas presents."

"Did you say presents?" I asked, not sure I'd heard him right. "I thought you were supposed to be the ghost of Christmas present, as in the here and now."

"Potato, potahto." He held out a chubby arm. "Shall we?"

"I'm good," I assured him, not wanting to do the whooshing thing again—ever. "I'm full of Christmas spirit. Really, I am. Deck the halls and figgy pudding and all that."

"The bare tree downstairs seems to tell a different story." Santa jutted out his arm impatiently. "I'm a busy spirit, you know. Don't have all night."

"Fine." I laid my hand on his arm and closed my eyes. It didn't help. We landed so hard, I nearly lost my footing. St. Nick steadied me.

"I think I'm going to throw up," I said.

"You won't," he assured me. "It only feels that way."

As I regained use of my vision, I blinked to bring my surroundings into focus. St. Nick and I stood in front of a small house decorated with twinkling lights. He stepped right through the door without opening it.

I stood on the porch, not about to walk through solid wood. A gloved hand emerged from the other side of the door and grabbed my arm, pulling me into the living room.

"Ouch." I shuddered, trying to shake off the feeling that my insides had been rearranged.

In the middle of the room, two couples sat around a table playing cards while three young children ran in and out of the room. An oversized tree stood in a corner of the room covered in handmade ornaments that I guessed had been created by the children, who shrieked with joy and excitement as they played. I covered my ears.

"Why do children have to be so loud?" I asked, not expecting an answer. "Also, where are we and who are these people?" I left out the follow up question—*why did you bring me here?*

"The Petersons live just a few blocks from you," St. Nick said. "Mr. Peterson—he's the older gentleman at the table—had to retire early due to his health. He's barely getting by, but you will notice that he managed to decorate the tree."

I ignored the barb. "Maybe you didn't know that I recently lost my mother. The first Christmas without a loved one is difficult, you know."

"True." St. Nick nodded in Mr. Peterson's direction. "He could tell you all about that."

We stood and watched as the two couples chatted about their lives and their plans for the holiday while I fidgeted, uncomfortable being an uninvited guest in a stranger's home.

As Mr. Peterson shuffled the deck he said, "Thank you all for being here. I never knew it would be so hard to get used to an empty house. I'm so grateful for all of you."

"We all miss Mary," the older woman said, forcing a smile as she blinked back a tear.

"Who's Mary?" I asked. "And where'd she go?" The moment I said the words I knew that Mr. Peterson was a widower.

I glanced back at the tree and felt my jaw drop. "That's my tree topper! These people are thieves!"

As I turned to St. Nick for an explanation, I grabbed his sleeve. Big mistake.

With a whoosh, my surroundings spun around me before fading to black and I may have passed out. As I came to, I recognized the community center. By the decorations, I could tell we were at the holiday event. At one end of the room, Santa Claus sat on a large red chair, with a petite older woman on his knee.

There was no comparison. "His beard is totally fake."

The ghostly St. Nick chuckled. "You mortals. You think you know what is fake and what isn't. Little do you know—"

"Irma!" I called out, laughing as I walked toward her. "What are you doing on Santa's lap? Trying to convince him you weren't naughty?"

"She can't hear you," the spirit said. "Your body is still back home on the sofa."

"Really?"

He shrugged. "I'm not sure. No one ever explained it to me. Maybe you're dreaming."

If no one could hear me, that meant I could eavesdrop and see what people said when I wasn't around. I spotted Jennifer talking with Dr. Fredeline Severs. Her friends, me included, called her Freddie.

"I'm worried about April," Jennifer was saying. "She didn't come to the tree lighting either. I brought home a tree and she said she'd decorate it, but I bet the next time I see it, it will still be bare."

"She'll be fine," Freddie said. "I remember the first Christmas without my dad. I didn't want to celebrate at all."

Jennifer got a faraway look in her eyes. "After my mom died, I pretended everything was okay. I plastered a smile on my face and did everything the way we did when she was alive. I thought it would make it easier on my dad, but I'm not sure it did."

"Everyone copes with loss their own way," Freddie said. "And we need to respect that."

"Oh." Jennifer frowned. "Do you think I've been too pushy?"

"No, no," Freddie reassured her. "April knows you have the best intentions."

Eavesdropping on my friends wasn't as much fun as I expected. I spotted Mayor Gasden talking with Mrs. Higglesworth and sidled up to them.

"Speaking of April May…" Mrs. Higglesworth began.

"Must we?" the mayor asked in a haughty tone.

Mrs. Higglesworth chuckled. "I, um, checked around, and it turns out that the finial she claimed to be a Michael André was a crudely made imitation."

"Crudely made?" How dare she insult my mother's handiwork like that. "And how did you know that, Mrs. Higglesworth?" I knew she couldn't hear me, but I kept talking. "Are you the one who stole it from me?"

But if she'd stolen it, then how had it ended up at Mr. Peterson's house?

I nearly grabbed St Nick's arm but stopped myself just in time. I wasn't ready to leave this party yet. "Mrs. Higglesworth and Mr. Peterson must be in on it together."

The ghost narrowed his eyes. "'In on it?' On what?"

"Stealing my tree topper. Maybe when Mrs. H. realized it wasn't valuable, she let her accomplice keep it."

I felt the spirit's disapproval as he shook his head. He held out his arm for me to take.

I put my hands on my hips. "Isn't there another way to travel? And where are we going now?"

"I'm taking you home."

"Thanks, I think I'll walk." It might take an hour or two, but it had to be better than his way.

"I'm afraid that's not possible, April."

Maybe his arm would get tired eventually. Or maybe he had someone else to haunt. All I had to do was outlast him.

After a minute or so I gave up. "Fine." I grabbed his arm and held on tightly.

THE GHOST OF CHRISTMAS FUTURE

When I came back to the real world, Whisk sat on the ottoman washing his paws. The ghosts from my dreams would probably fade completely from my memory by the morning.

"It's good to be back in the real world, Whisk," I said. "You have no idea—"

"Oh good. You're back," the cat interrupted. "Hello."

I sat straight up. "Did you say something?"

"Yes. I said hello." His whiskers twitched as he spoke. "I believe the proper response is to return my greeting and possibly inquire about my health."

I stared at the cat dumbfounded. "Hello, Whisk," I managed to say. "How are you?"

"Quite well, thank you." He stretched, arching his back, then lay down, his eyes firmly fixed on me. "Although I must admit, I'm not entirely satisfied with the meals you've been serving of late. I wonder if you might consider adding something fresh—tuna perhaps? I haven't had tuna in ages." The cat licked his lips.

I rubbed my eyes and leaned closer to see if the cat's mouth moved when he spoke.

"Have you figured it out?" he asked.

"Figured out how you can talk all of a sudden?"

"Don't be silly. Cats can't talk."

"You lost me there."

Whisk jumped onto the sofa next to me. "I am the ghost of Christmas future. Tomorrow, sadly, I will no longer be able to communicate with you in this way. So... tuna?"

"Um, sure." I had a few questions, but I started with, "So you're Whisk and also the ghost of Christmas future, and that's why you can temporarily communicate?"

"Close enough." Whisk held out a paw. "Shall we?"

I took a deep breath and blew it out slowly. "Might as well get this over with." I touched his furry leg, hoping this would be the last whoosh of the night. As the room spun, I felt a wave of nausea.

We landed more softly this time. Perhaps Whisk had given me some of his cat powers, allowing me to touch down lightly. Or, more likely, I was in the middle of one of the strangest dreams I'd ever had where the rules of physics didn't apply.

Within moments, I recognized our surroundings and grinned. The undulating blue, green, and violet lights of the Mermaid Café surrounded me. Irma's restaurant was one of my favorite places in the entire world. I grinned when I spotted Jennifer but stopped smiling when she walked by with tears streaming down her face.

"What's wrong, Jennifer?" I called out, but of course she couldn't hear me.

She ran up to Freddie and threw her arms around her. "I can't believe she's gone."

"I know, I know," Freddie said in a soothing tone patting her on her back. When Jennifer released her hold, she added, "I thought she was indestructible."

"Me too." Following Freddie's gaze, I saw the casket in the middle of the room. She handed Jennifer a tissue, which she used to wipe her eyes and blow her nose.

"I'm sorry I haven't called since your wedding," Jennifer said. "I keep meaning to…"

"I know." Freddie managed a smile. "I'm glad you could make it back for the funeral. Or I should say wake. She never wanted a funeral."

"Who died?" I raised my voice as if they were hard of hearing. I looked down at Whisk. "Is this my funeral?" but he didn't answer.

"I'm sorry it took a funeral to bring us all back to Serenity Cove," Jennifer said. "Ever since I moved to New York, I keep thinking I'll fly home. But with April gone…"

"Me too," Freddie agreed.

"Gone?" I asked Freddie who still couldn't hear me. "Where have I gone?" I turned to Whisk, demanding, "Am I dead?"

Whisk rubbed against my leg. "This is a possible future, April. Not the only future."

I couldn't take my eyes off the casket. The top panel stood open, and I slowly walked toward it, my heart beating faster and faster.

Irma lay on white silk, her walking stick tucked in next to her. She looked as if she might sit up and say, "April fool's!" any moment. I reached out to touch her arm but pulled my hand away at the last moment.

"What year is it?" I asked Whisk.

He did the cat version of a shrug. "I've never

really kept track of time in the way you two-leggeds do."

I followed Jennifer and Freddie to the bar where a bartender handed them glasses of champagne to toast their friend. How much had the two of them aged? Two years? Ten?

Whisk jumped up on the bar and sniffed at a bowl of peanuts. "Time to go, April."

"Already? But I haven't found out how Irma died or where I went off to. Why would I leave the most wonderful friends I've ever had in my entire life?"

Whisk reached out a paw, but I ignored him, straining to hear what Jennifer and Freddie were saying.

"I can't believe April didn't come," Jennifer said. "I thought she cared about Irma. I thought she cared about us."

"I do," I yelled. "I do care!"

Before I realized it, Whisk put his paw on my arm, and I felt the now familiar whoosh.

A NEW DAY DAWNS

I awoke in my own bed, not sure how I'd gotten there. Slipping out from the covers, I went to the window and pulled the curtains aside.

The early morning sun glistened on the waves, seagulls squawked overhead, and a few fluffy clouds floated by. A quick look at my phone confirmed the date. Christmas Eve Day.

After slipping into the same clothes I'd worn the day before, I hurried downstairs to take another look at the still bare tree. Before I decorated it, I wanted to visit someone.

Mrs. Higglesworth.

Not even taking time to make coffee, I jumped into my car and drove straight to City Hall, which shared the building with the community center and the police station. I headed straight for the mayor's office.

Pauline jumped when I barged through the door. "Oh my." She giggled nervously. "You startled me."

"I want to see the mayor," I demanded.

Pauline's eyes widened, perhaps not used to me being so stern. "She's taking a few days off. She'll be back on Tuesday. Would you like to make an appointment?" She reached for her book.

It couldn't wait until Tuesday. In a softer tone, I asked, "Do you know Mrs. Higglesworth? I need to get in touch with her."

Pauline shook her head. "I can't give out that information, April. I could get fired."

"Oh, right. Of course." I wracked my brain, thinking of how to find the woman. "I'm having a few people over this evening for a little Christmas Eve party. I know it's very last minute, but if you don't have plans, I'd love to have you join us."

Her face lit up. "I'd love to. What can I bring?"

"Just yourself. I was going to ask Mrs. Higglesworth and her assistant, Miss Paisley. I hope they have plans for the evening. I hate for anyone to be alone at this time of year."

Pauline's smile returned. "I'll give her a call and invite them both for you."

"Thank you!" With a quick goodbye and a "Merry Christmas," I hurried back to my car. Not feeling confident that Mrs. Higglesworth would come to my party, I had another idea how to find her—by talking to her accomplice.

After a half hour of driving up and down every street in Serenity Cove looking for Mr. Peterson's house, I nearly gave up.

"This is ridiculous," I muttered. Why was I driving around looking for a house from a dream? Mr. Peterson and his family were figments of my overactive imagination. Probably a result of watching too many versions of *A Christmas Carol.*

Still, I couldn't resist turning down one more street. I spotted the little house and gasped. "It is real."

Pulling up in front of the house, I told myself not to get excited. I must have driven by the house one day and incorporated it into my dream. That didn't mean there was anyone named Peterson living there.

Only one way to find out. I walked up the pathway to the front door and knocked.

Mr. Peterson opened the door. "Hello." When I didn't respond, he added, "May I help you?"

"I'm April May." I should have rehearsed what else to say. "You might think I'm crazy, but I think you have a tree topper that belongs to me."

He nodded. "Come in."

I stepped into the room which looked exactly as I'd remembered. There in the corner, on top of the tree, stood my mother's creation. Mr. Peterson reached up and carefully removed it.

"My grandson's not going to be happy to see it gone," he said as he gently handed it to me. "Archie's said he got it in the trash. He loves digging for treasure—that's what he calls it. He was so excited when he came home with this. But I'm guessing you didn't put it in the trash."

My mind tried to put the pieces together. Had Archie come into my house and stolen the tree topper?

"How tall is Archie?" I hoped he'd take my question in stride.

His eyebrows rose slightly but held his hand out chest high. "About so. He's eight."

Archie never could have reached the top of my tree—Jennifer barely managed. I smiled. "I don't know how it ended up in the trash, but that must be where he got it. I last saw it on the top of a six-foot tree." Whoever had stolen it from my tree must have quickly realized it was nearly worthless, at least to anyone except me. "It only has sentimental value, but I would like to offer a reward. If it wasn't for your grandson, it would have ended up at the dump, never to be seen again."

"That's very kind, but we couldn't accept a reward."

I tried to convince him, but he stood his ground. As I turned to go, I couldn't help thinking his house seemed very quiet. "Where are your grandchildren now?"

"They went back to Milwaukee," he said, walking me to the door. "They'll be spending Christmas Day with my daughter-in-law's family. It's tough having to share them."

"Especially this year," I said, not thinking. I quickly added, "I lost my mother and I've been having a tough time getting through this first Christmas without her."

"I'm sure it will get easier," he said, adding, "It has to."

I stared at the tree topper in my hand. "I'll never stop missing her, but sometimes I feel her presence, like she's watching over me."

He nodded, his eyes shiny with unshed tears. "I know what you mean."

"Mr. Peterson, do you have plans for this evening?"

"Please call me Joe. And no, I don't have plans. Why do you ask?"

"I'm having several friends over to my house for Christmas Eve. Nothing formal, just drinks and snacks and maybe we'll play some games. You should come."

"I'd like that," he said. "You live in the old Thornly house, don't you? SereniTea Tearoom?"

"That's the place."

With little time to waste, I hurried home, climbing the steps to the attic to search for more decorations. There were several lovely old ornaments in the box Jennifer had brought down earlier, but I needed more. Much more.

Back in my car, I drove to Somerton and headed straight for the pet store, where I bought Whisk's new bed, a catnip mouse, and several cans of tuna. I popped into one of the shops on Main Street and emerged with three bags overflowing with decorations. My last stop was the grocery store, where I bought enough food and drinks for an army.

On the way back home, I called Freddie, Irma, and Jennifer to invite them over for a Christmas Eve party, telling them to bring any guests they wished. Freddie asked if she could bring a date and I smiled, wondering if I'd be meeting her future husband.

When I carried all my packages into the house, I had a feeling I was forgetting someone. I didn't want anyone in town to spend their Christmas Eve alone.

Deputy Bonner! I called the police station and left a message for him to join us. I didn't know if he'd be on duty or had plans, but I wanted to make sure he knew he was welcome.

I strung lights on the tree and hung two dozen little teacup ornaments on the branches, along with a ceramic tiger that reminded me of Whisk. On the top, I carefully placed my mother's creation. It was a work of art after all—not by a famous artist, but by a woman who often fell short fulfilling the demands of being a mother. Her love made up for her shortcomings in the end.

I plugged the lights in and stepped back to admire the tree. Perfect. All it needed was some presents underneath. I wrapped Whisk's bed and placed it under the tree, disappointed in myself for not thinking to get presents for anyone else.

When I finished decorating the front room, including long strands of greenery woven up the banisters, I plugged in the lights—there were at least a dozen strings around the room.

The effect was magical, with twinkling lights reflecting off the chandelier crystals. After admiring my handiwork, I glanced at my watch. Time to start cooking and baking.

Chef looked up when I entered the kitchen. "Ah, there you are. And the smile has returned to your face. Have you found *ton esprit de Noël*?"

It seemed I'd heard him use that phrase before, but I didn't waste time trying to remember. I went straight for the three cookbooks he'd written when he'd been alive and running his own restaurant. "I could use your help planning my Christmas Eve feast."

He grinned. "A feast is my specialty. Let us begin."

CHRISTMAS EVE FEAST

While the food baked and simmered, I decorated martini glasses, dipping the rims in white frosting and adding sprinkles.

Irma was the first to arrive. She stepped inside the door and stood speechless. "Did the Christmas fairies come and transform your house?"

I hurried to greet her and threw my arms around her tiny body.

"Eek!" she yelped.

I let go. "Sorry if I squeezed too hard."

She tried to hide her smile. "What has gotten into you?"

"Christmas spirit. Or I should say spirits."

"Oh, I see. Drinking again."

I laughed. "Not yet, but I made two big batches of eggnog—one with rum and one without. Not only that, but I'm offering special holiday-inspired cocktails. What can I get you?"

"I'll take a glass of eggnog. *With* the rum." She breathed in the aromas wafting from the kitchen. "Whatever you're cooking, I'll take some of that too."

"Hors d'oeuvres are coming right up."

The doorbell rang and I asked Irma to answer it. "That might be Joe Peterson."

"You invited Joe?" Her eyebrows pulled together. "Since when do you know him?"

I grinned. "Since yesterday. He seemed lonely, so I asked him to join us. His wife passed away recently…"

"That was very thoughtful of you," she said, heading for the door while I ducked into the kitchen.

When I returned with their drinks and a tray of cranberry brie bites, *boulettes de viands,* and smoked salmon canapes, Irma sat in front of the fireplace while Joe lit the fire. The two of them were chatting up a storm.

"Where are the cheese puffs?" Irma asked, adding to Joe, "April is famous for her cheese puffs."

"They're coming." I set the food and drinks on

the coffee table. "I hope you don't mind me leaving you for a bit longer."

Joe grinned. "Not at all."

Freddie and Jennifer arrived next. I emerged from the kitchen with a bright red pomegranate sparkler for Jennifer, and a peppermint martini for Freddie. After ducking back into the kitchen, I returned with more food, including my popular cheese puffs.

"Don't eat too much," I warned. "I've got a traditional English prime rib dinner coming up. It has a bit of a French twist."

"Everything April makes has a French twist," Jennifer explained. "She has a crush on the chef who lived here sixty years ago."

"I do not." I felt my cheeks redden.

"The moment she saw his picture on the back of his cookbook, it was love at first sight," she said with a laugh.

I hoped Chef couldn't hear us talking from the kitchen. What would he think?

As I got ready to put the Yorkshire puddings in the oven, the doorbell rang again, and I went into the front room to greet the new arrivals.

Jennifer opened the door for Mrs. Higglesworth and Miss Jane Paisley, who were dressed much the same as they had been when I first met them. Today, Mrs. Higglesworth's suit was burgundy, a color that suited her much better than gray. Jane wore a red cardigan with green holly embroidered on the front.

I watched them as they entered. Mrs. H's eyes went straight to the tree in the corner. She didn't appear surprised to see the topper in place, but she did turn up her nose as if in disdain.

Jane's eyes widened when she saw the tree, and she quickly looked away, telling me everything I wanted to know.

After welcoming them both, I gave what I hoped was a contrite smile. "I wanted to apologize for the other day."

"Apologize?" Mrs. H's eyebrows rose slightly. "Whatever for?"

"I should have told you right away that my mother had made the tree topper that you'd mistaken for a Michael André. How did you figure out it hadn't been created by a famous artist?"

Her cheeks reddened. "I, well..." she began, then huffed. "Fine. I took a picture when no one was looking. After zooming in, it was obvious it wasn't genuine. I will admit I was fooled for a moment." She strolled over to the tree. "It's obviously created by an unknown and fledgling artist."

I grinned. “That may be, but it’s one of a kind, and I love it.”

Jane hovered by the others who sat in front of the fireplace. I couldn’t accuse her in front of everyone on Christmas Eve. But it didn’t seem right to let her get away with theft, either.

“Miss Paisley,” I said as I took her arm. “Would you mind helping me in the kitchen?”

Jennifer jumped up. “I can help.”

“Thanks, but we’ve got it.”

Jane stiffened as I guided her into the kitchen.

I popped the Yorkshire puddings in the oven, set the timer, then turned to face her. “Why did you steal my tree topper?”

She tried to look shocked or insulted, but failed on both counts. “I don’t know what you’re talking about,” she said, her voice shaky.

“The only reason it’s back on the tree is because someone found it in the trash, and it managed to make its way back to me. That tree topper is one of the few things that I have of my mother’s. We didn’t have much growing up, so I don’t have any family heirlooms to remember her by.”

“I’m sorry to hear that, but I don’t know what it has to do with me.” She stared at the door as if planning her escape. “Besides, you seem to be doing just fine now, with your big house and your tearoom." Bitterness had crept into her voice, and I wondered what life had done to her to put such a large chip on her shoulder.

The timer rang at the same time as the doorbell. I pulled the Yorkshire puddings out of the oven and went into the front room.

"Wait here, please," I told Jane. "I'll be right back." I wasn't done talking with her.

Deputy Bonner had arrived, still dressed in his uniform. I hurried to welcome him.

"I hope you don't mind me coming to your party dressed like this," he told me. "I didn't have time to change."

"Not at all," I said. "In fact, I wonder if you might do me a favor."

I explained in a whisper as I led him to the kitchen. "There's a woman in my kitchen who I believe took my tree topper last night. If you give her one of your dominating stares, maybe her guilty conscience will get her to confess." When we entered, Jane froze, staring at the deputy with wide eyes.

Deputy Bonner said nothing, simply stood with his hands on his hips as he towered over her. I took a deep breath as the tension in the room thickened.

"Fine!" Jane blurted out. "Fine! I stole the stupid ornament. When *she* started talking about how valuable it was, I saw my chance. Do you have any idea what it's like working for someone like her? Never a thank you, never a day off, never a vacation! But what was the point in asking for time off—she didn't pay me enough to go anywhere. She's a stingy Scrooge!"

We all turned, following a sound behind us. Mrs. H. stood in the doorway, and by the look on her face, I knew she'd heard everything.

"Come along, Jane," she said and left the room, the door swinging behind her.

"I'm so sorry," Jane said, grabbing my hand. "If I'd known how important it was to you, I never would have taken it. I just thought—you have so many nice things. Maybe you wouldn't miss one." She turned to Deputy Bonner. "Am I under arrest?"

He gestured to me. "It depends if Ms. May wants to press charges."

Part of me wanted to see her go to jail so that she'd learn her lesson. I wasn't sure she regretted anything other than getting caught. Spending Christmas Eve in a jail cell might give her time to consider her choices, but I couldn't do it.

I shook my head. "I'm not going to have you arrested on Christmas Eve."

Mrs. H's voice carried from the other room. "Jane?"

Jane's eye twitched. She squeezed my hand gently, then let it go. "Thank you, April."

"Jane!" The voice bellowed.

"I don't have any right to ask you this, but…" Jane hesitated. "Do you think I could stay at your party?" Her expression was as hopeful as a child on Christmas morning.

"Of course," I said, surprised by the request. "You're more than welcome."

She bit her lip and blinked back tears before stepping back into the front room. I followed her, wanting to see how she would handle her boss.

"Finally," Mrs. H. muttered. "We're leaving."

"I'm not," Jane said. "I'm staying here."

"Really? After what you did? Well, I suppose that's your business." She gave Jane a withering stare. "I'll see you on Monday."

"No, I'm afraid you won't." Jane's voice, now steady, was full of determination. "I quit."

Mrs. H's mouth dropped open for a moment before she clamped it shut. "Well!" Her mouth puckered into a frown. "We can talk about this later." She pushed the front door open and walked out, letting the screen door slam shut behind her.

Jane looked about to collapse, so I led her to a chair.

"Eggnog?" I asked. "Or maybe champagne is more in order, since it sounds like you've just made a life-altering decision."

Jane blinked and looked into my face, still stunned from her impulsive action. "I just quit my job. What am I going to do now?"

"Eat, drink and be merry," I said. "You'll figure it out later. Right now, it's Christmas Eve, and time to celebrate."

When we'd finished our feast, I leaned back in my chair, too full to get up and carry the plates to our kitchen.

Jane jumped to her feet. "I'll clear the table."

Jennifer offered to help and the two of them soon cleared the table. Jennifer returned carrying a *bûche de Noël,* the traditional Christmas cake in the shape of a log. Jane followed behind with coffee.

"I can't believe how beautifully you decorated the tearoom," Jennifer said as she sliced the cake and handed out servings. "I half expected the tree to still be bare when I got here this evening. I'm glad you found your Christmas spirit."

"Funny story," I said. "I had a crazy dream last night."

I told them about Charles Dickens taking me to my childhood home and St. Nick showing me Mr. Peterson's house and the community center.

"Who was the ghost of Christmas future?" Irma asked.

I chuckled. "It was Whisk."

At that moment, a meow came from the stairs, and we all turned to see the cat sitting on the landing. He nonchalantly licked his paws.

"Did you enjoy the tuna?" I explained to the others. "In the dream, Whisk complained about the food I'd been giving him and asked for tuna. I figured it couldn't hurt. Besides, it's Christmas Eve."

"Hold on," Mr. Peterson said. "You say you visited my house in your dream?"

"Yes, and it looked just the way it did when you invited me in earlier today."

"But how is that possible?" he asked. "You've never been there before. And the tree topper—did you see that in your dream too?"

I hadn't thought of that. How did I know the tree topper sat on top of his tree if I hadn't actually been there? I shrugged. "I can't explain it."

I hurried to the kitchen for another bottle of champagne, but I really wanted a quiet moment to think. Chef stood in the corner with a glass of red wine in his hand.

"Something wrong?" Chef asked. "You look as if you've seen a ghost."

I began laughing and had to force myself to

stop. "I've seen several ghosts lately. You'd think by now I'd take it in stride."

"You would think I would get used to seeing you every day in my kitchen, and yet every time you enter, I find I am surprised." He smiled, leading me to believe he found it to be a pleasant surprise.

"Thank you for helping me find my Christmas spirit."

"I am glad you are not so sad now with the long face," he said. "I much prefer to see your lovely smile."

"Happy Christmas Eve, Chef Emile." I blew him a kiss and, if I wasn't mistaken, he blushed.

I returned to the group and filled their flutes. "I'd like to make a toast."

Irma grinned. "I think Tiny has something to say."

Mr. Peterson looked around the room confused. "Tiny?"

"Yes," Irma said. "Deputy Timothy Bonner. We call him Tiny."

I chuckled, finally putting the pieces together. "Of course—Tiny Tim. I guess you were meant to be here tonight."

Tiny stood and raised his glass. "God bless us, every one."

SNOWBALL COOKIES

INGREDIENTS:

- 1 cup unsalted butter, softened
- 6 Tablespoons powdered sugar
- 1 teaspoon vanilla
- 2 cups all-purpose flour
- ¾ cup finely chopped pecans or other chopped nuts (such as walnuts or almonds) - optional
- ¼ teaspoon salt (omit if using salted butter)
- Additional powdered sugar for rolling cookies in (about 1 cup)

DIRECTIONS:

1. Heat oven to 350 degrees F.
2. Use a big spoon (preferably wooden) to cream the butter with the powdered sugar and vanilla
3. Stir in flour, salt, and optional nuts, and mix until the dough holds together
4. Shape into one-inch balls and place one inch apart on ungreased cookie sheet
5. Bake 10 to 12 minutes – they won't be brown except on the bottom. Let cool for 10-15 minutes on a wire rack.
6. Roll warm cookies in powdered sugar and allow to cool.
7. Roll in powdered sugar again.

April's Note: When I say "finely" chopped nuts, I mean it! They're wonderful without nuts, too. Or, for a festive surprise, crush red and green candy canes and mix them in instead of the nuts.

ABOUT THE AUTHOR

Karen Sue Walker is a mystery author who believes in justice and happy endings!

She loves afternoon tea, crafting, cooking, baking, and making new friends.

Would you like to sign up for emails that will bring a smile to your face and warmth to your soul? At the very least, you'll surely enjoy regular pictures of Kit the Chipooshi (Chihuahua, Poodle, Shih Tzu mix)!

Visit karensuewalker.com now and sign up!

To see the entire Haunted Tearoom Mystery Series in order, visit the Amazon series page.

ALSO BY KAREN SUE WALKER

Haunted Tearoom Cozy Mysteries

Tea is for Trouble

Tea is for Toxin

Tea is for Tragedy

Tea is for Tarot

Tea is for Traitor

Tea is for Tears

Tea is for Temptation

Tea is for Taken (December 2023)

Tea is for Talisman (2024)

Bridal Shop Cozy Mysteries

Charming Small-Town Mysteries with Heart

Murder in White Lace

Murder in Crimson Velvet

Murder in Blue Gingham

Murder in Lavender Silk

Murder in Pink Taffeta

Printed in Great Britain
by Amazon

36597896R00098